DEFENDER

ALSO BY GRAHAM McNAMEE

Acceleration
Beyond
Bonechiller

DEFENDER

GRAHAM McNAMEE

WENDY
LAMB
BOOKS

Text copyright © 2016 by Graham McNamee
Jacket art copyright © 2016 by Trevillion Images

All rights reserved. Published in the United States by Wendy Lamb Books, an imprint of Random House Children's Books, a division of Penguin Random House LLC, New York.

Wendy Lamb Books and the colophon are trademarks of Penguin Random House LLC.

Visit us on the Web! randomhouseteens.com

Educators and librarians, for a variety of teaching tools, visit us at RHTeachersLibrarians.com

Library of Congress Cataloging-in-Publication Data
McNamee, Graham.
Defender / Graham McNamee. — First edition.
pages cm
Summary: Seventeen-year-old Tyne and her boyfriend Stick investigate a decades-old murder after she finds the body of a girl in the basement wall of her apartment building.
ISBN 978-0-553-49895-0 (trade) — ISBN 978-0-553-49896-7 (lib. bdg.) — ISBN 978-0-553-49898-1 (pbk.) — ISBN 978-0-553-49897-4 (ebook)
[1. Mystery and detective stories. 2. Murder—Fiction.
3. Dating (Social customs)—Fiction.] I. Title.
PZ7.M4787934De 2016 [Fic]—dc23
2015010242

The text of this book is set in 11-point Bembo.
Jacket design by Tom Sanderson
Interior design by Patrice Sheridan

Printed in the United States of America
10 9 8 7 6 5 4 3 2 1
First Edition

DEFENDER

NEVER TELL

1

"ATTACK OR RETREAT? Do I shoot, or shake you?" Dad says. "What's my next move, girl? Read me."

He stares at me across the little back alley basketball court behind our building. He's got the ball, but I'm between him and the hoop.

"Whatever you try, old man, I'll smack it down."

He laughs. Dad's my trainer. He's big, but I'm bigger. I play center on my high school team, and I'm a monster. Six feet six inches tall.

They've got a lot of names for me—Girlzilla, Bigfoot, Titanic. But mostly they call me Tiny. Because my real name is Tyne, and they think it's funny.

"What's my move?" He dribbles just out of reach. A bear of a guy, with shaggy brown hair, a stubbly beard and a growly voice.

It's after dark, deep in December. You can see our breath in the cold air as we work up a sweat, playing by the parking lot lights. The hoop is bolted to the wall.

"Don't watch the ball," Dad says. "It won't tell you. Not my eyes either—the eyes will trick you, looking one way when I go the other. I can fake you out with my shoulders, head, hands."

He shows me the fakes, making me bite every time.

"Where do I look, then?"

"Right here." He pats his gut. "The belly button. Body can't go anywhere without it. Where it goes, the rest follows. So, read me now."

Dad runs through a sequence of fakes, getting me to twitch but not commit to his moves. I wait till his gut twists, giving him away, and then I'm there to cut him off.

"Not bad." He backs up. "Remember, keep low. Knees bent, on your toes, butt down, arms out. How's the knee feeling?"

"Sore, but not screaming."

I'm a wounded warrior. Got injured in a game, and now I'm wearing a brace on my right knee till it heals.

"Take it slow and steady. We'll get you back in the game."

It's crunch time for me in the push to score a college scholarship. I'm seventeen, and this is my senior year. The scouts are watching, looking for prospects, and I can't let them think I'm damaged goods.

So we have our after-school practices here, with Dad showing me what he picked up playing hoops himself, and we focus on the key defense drills—the moves and footwork. *It's a dance,* he likes to say.

"You had enough?" Dad asks.

"You're the one huffing and puffing."

I breathe deep, the chilled air a fresh shock to my lungs. These are the dying days of the year, but winter hasn't really hit us yet. The city wakes to morning frosts but stays sunny and mild, with no snow. Feels like the calm before the storm.

"You talk trash." He grins. "Can you back it up?"

"Try me."

He retreats, eyes shining in the darkness where the lights don't reach. I crouch low, waiting for him to make his move. We face off for a long moment, the seconds counting down to the beat of the bouncing ball.

Then he charges. Straight at me, before twisting right. I get there before him, but he pivots, spinning left to pass. I back up quick to stay with him, and just as he goes in for the layup I bang into him, swatting away the ball. We slam together and I get knocked off-balance. I lose my feet and start to go down, but Dad catches me. We stagger in each other's arms, and he turns before we crash into the wall so he takes the impact.

Dad grunts, the wind knocked out of him. We separate and he hunches over.

"You okay?" he pants.

I nod, gasping.

"That was . . . a foul, girl."

"No way," I say. "Clean block."

"You play dirty."

"I get it from you."

He laughs, breathless.

We call it a night. I hunt down the ball in the shadows; then we make our way to the back door, winded and stumbling, leaning together to keep each other up.

A dance in the dark with my old man.

2

I **WAKE UP** to the end of the world.

My bed shaking, the room quaking. The deafening noise of concrete cracking.

My eyes fly open. I try to focus and see if the walls are splitting open, and the ceiling is collapsing on me.

My little brother is bouncing on my mattress, while the roar of the road crew tearing up the street outside thunders loud.

I fight to catch my breath.

Just another day here. Not the end of the world, only feels that way.

"Quit it, Squirrel," I say. We call my brother that because he's always climbing, pouncing and bouncing—like now.

I go to kick him off, but stop. Reaching down beside my bed, I grab a basketball off the floor.

"Go fetch." I toss the ball out the door of my room.

As he chases after it, I get up and lock the door. Stumbling over to the window, I open it for a breath of chilly air, and get blasted by the wrecking crew twenty-five floors below. We live in downtown Toronto at the top of a slum tower they call the Zoo. I stare out at the view, still expecting something apocalyptic. But there are no bombed-out buildings, mushroom clouds or giant meteors in the sky. Those wandering figures in shredded clothes down there aren't the undead rising, just homeless people turned out from the shelter down the street.

And it's a gorgeous sunny day, freaky fine weather for early winter.

You'd think the city workers would get the week off from construction chaos. But it's December 27 and they're back at it with their Christmas break quake.

I stretch out as much as I can in my small room. But it's a tight squeeze for a giant with my reach. From fingertip to fingertip I've got a wingspan not far off seven feet. I take a size fourteen men's sneaker. And my weight—never mind. I'm *big*.

My phone buzzes from somewhere in my sheets. I dig it out and find a text from my guy, Stick. He's known as Stick because he's a skinny twig of a dude.

The message says: Rise and shine, Tyne. HOLIDAZE CRAZE! Let's run naked in the streets. Set this town on fire!

And there's a shot of Stick with his eyes bugged, spiky curls sticking straight out, mouth wide in a silent shout—looking like somebody just tased his testicles.

I text back: Arson + Indecent Exposure? Count me in. But breakfast first.

We're free for another week, so I'm up for anything.

I turn and trip over my discarded knee brace, wincing at the stab of pain that shoots up my right leg. I grab the bottle of painkillers on my desk and pop one. During a game, I got a minor tear in my MCL, the ligament that holds the knee together. I've been sidelined for weeks. I'm trying to cut back on the pills so I don't get hooked, just one in the morning to get me started and one at night so I can sleep.

I limp down the hall to the bathroom, keeping an eye out for Squirrel attacks, and shut the door.

"You again," I grunt at my reflection in the mirror. I'm not a big fan of my face. There's too much of everything: wide brow, long nose, square jaw. I've got the bone structure of a Viking giant. I keep my black hair long because I get mistaken for a guy way too much. They never see *me,* just my size. But I like my eyes. They're leaf green, a warm summer color, and they contrast with my dark brows and thick eyelashes. Stick calls them emerald, says they light up like green fire. He's my kind of crazy.

Dad customized the shower so I can fit. He's almost as tall as me, so he understands. When you're freaky big you've got to be a contortionist to fit into this world.

I turn on the hot to ease the stiffness in my knee, but I'm blasted with freezing-cold water. I gasp, frantically twisting the hot faucet and getting only ice. Nothing ever works in this dump.

I do a quick arctic rinse, grab a towel and rub some

warmth back into my goose-bumped flesh, then pull on my pajama bottoms and T-shirt.

I run into Dad in the hallway, carrying his toolbox.

"Good, you're up," he says.

"Up and frozen."

"Hot water's out."

"Little late on the update." I shiver, my hair dripping icicles down my neck.

"We've got a broken pipe in the basement. Major flooding. And a partial power outage, with two of the elevators out of order. So I'm going to need you, honey."

"No way."

Dad's the superintendent of our building, and when everything's falling apart—as usual—I have to help.

Slum slave, that's me.

"I'm on break," I tell him. "No school, no work, no nothing."

"I just need you for an hour, tops. Then you're free. Pay you double."

I want to say no. But he's got a monster of a job, and I can't leave him hanging.

"One hour, then I'm gone."

"That's my girl."

"More like your helper monkey."

The basketball I tossed for Squirrel lies on the floor between us. Dad puts down his toolbox and picks it up.

"Maybe we can work on your free throws later. Gotta improve your shooting percentage." He bounces the ball between his legs, shifting and shuffling his feet like he's going to blast past me for a basket. "Show the scouts you can hit your foul shots."

Dad's my motivator and superfan, dreaming up a life for me beyond this place. Not many Zoo grunts like me make it out and go to college.

But right now it's just a dream. So I'm stuck with janitor duty. He gives me the flood in the basement to clean up.

"It's all in the wrist." He passes me the ball.

"What, mopping or shooting?"

"Both, honey."

He scoops up his toolbox and gives me a scratchy stubble-kiss on the cheek as he squeezes by.

I dribble the ball through the living room, where Squirrel is arguing with the TV.

In the kitchen, Mom's getting her heart started with her first cup of coffee. They call her Red, because her hair is flaming. She's so petite you'd never guess she's popped out two kids, especially a beast like me.

"You look blue," she says.

"Ice bath."

I set the ball on the counter, and she watches me mix up my morning protein shake in the blender.

"Dad's got me on flood watch. On Christmas break."

"What can I say? That's life."

I think about that as I fire up the blender. Mom's always a morning grouch, because she works late nights as a waitress over at Shooters, a local sports bar.

"That's helpful." I gulp my chocolate-banana smoothie.

"Hey, if you want wisdom, wait till I wake up." She gives me a sleepy smile, a little hug and a pat on the butt to send me on my way.

■

THE ONLY WORKING elevator takes forever. When the doors finally open, I have to watch out because the elevators are usually out of sync with the floor by about a foot.

On four, old lady Celia joins me. At ninety-one years old, she's been living here forever. I hold the doors and give her a hand so she can make the step down using her cane. She moves in slow motion, with an artificial hip and both knees replaced (*but the boobs are still real,* she likes to joke).

"Thanks, supergirl. You know there's no heat? I could make ice cubes on my radiator. What kind of place are you running here?"

"More like it's running us. A pipe broke. We're working on it."

"Well, I'm going out to warm my bones in the sun." She looks me up and down in my work gear. "You won't be needing those rain boots. It's a beauty of a day."

"Not where I'm headed."

The elevator stops and Celia makes her creaky way out into a lobby flooded with sunshine. I feel like escaping into the sweet daylight.

But then the doors slam shut.

Taking me down.

3

I WADE INTO the flooded furnace room and turn on the pump to start draining the water through a hose that empties into a sink across the hall.

The tremors from the demolition work to replace the city's old sewer lines have been shaking our foundation and breaking pipes all over the place.

So here I am, Ghetto Cinderella, cleaning up her dungeon. Another half hour and I'll trade these rain boots for some glass sneakers—and go party.

The motor on the pump echoes loudly, thudding off the walls. *Thump thump thump.* I wander down the hall to get away from the noise and the damp, but the thumping follows, vibrating the air like the building's heartbeat.

My cell phone buzzes with a message from Stick:
You done yet? Let's do lunch. I need to feed!!!

The shot he sends with it shows him sucking in his nonexistent gut so you can count his ribs. No matter how much he eats, he stays stick skinny.

I start to text him back.

But then I stumble over something. There's a pile of crumbled plaster and concrete on the floor. I look up and see big cracks running up the wall around the door to the old incinerator room.

Since the road crew started ripping up the street, the quakes have wrecked more than the plumbing. No real structural damage, just surface stuff that Dad patches up. But this is the worst yet. These cracks are wide enough to fit my fingers in. Feels like we're living in a house of cards that could come crashing down any day.

I should check to see if there's more damage inside the room, and tell Dad. We're always on disaster patrol.

The incinerator room holds the huge furnace where they used to burn the trash. There was a garbage chute, with drawers opening on all twenty-five floors where you'd dump in anything burnable. The furnace was shut down decades ago, and the chute sealed up, with all the drawers plastered over. Nothing but spiders and dust in that room now.

I pull out my copy of the building's master key. The lock sticks, it's been so long since anyone tried it. Even after I rattle the knob till my key turns, the door's still jammed and I have to shoulder it open.

I find the switch on the wall inside. Nothing—the bulb must be blown.

Whenever Dad sends me on one of these jobs I bring a fanny pack with a mini tool kit—screwdriver, wrench, pliers and a small flashlight. The flashlight's thin beam shows me the hulking black furnace built into the wall on my left, with its door clamped shut. There's a shovel leaning against the smoke-stained wall beside it. They used the shovel to feed trash to the fire. A wooden chair sits forgotten in the middle of the room.

The floor is covered in a thick skin of dust, and each step I take sends up a powdery cloud, motes drifting in the flashlight's beam. Through some kind of weird acoustic trick in the basement I can hear the water pump's beat filling the room like an echo chamber.

There's a faint smell in the air, something bad. It always stinks down here, with mold everywhere and mushrooms sprouting in the darkest corners. We find the occasional dead rat, and you get slobs using the stairwells as urinals.

Scanning my light away from the furnace to the back wall, I catch sight of something. What is that?

A major crack in the wall stretches from the ceiling halfway to the floor, opening up a big hole. Chunks of concrete and plaster are scattered around. The crack looks new, with fresh scrapes in the dust where the debris has fallen.

As I go for a closer look, the rotten smell gets stronger. I aim my light into the hole and see that it opens onto a shaft that shoots up behind the wall. This must be the garbage chute that emptied out near the furnace, where the trash bags would pile up on the floor before getting shoveled into the flames.

Shining the light beam down, I spot something stuck at the bottom of the shaft.

A dusty garbage bag is stuffed in there. Looks like it was torn open by the falling concrete, with what's inside now spilling out.

My little light barely penetrates the blackness. But it shows me—

It's like something from a butcher shop. I make out a rib cage. Might be a whole animal carcass dumped in there, split open down the middle and hollowed out. How did that get here? The whole chute was emptied before they sealed it.

No way I'm cleaning this up. Not touching that.

Shifting the beam up the ribs, I see—

What is—

Oh God! No! No!

It's a face! A face! A human face!

I can't move. Can't look away. Shocked stiff.

The skin is shriveled tight to the skull. Closed eyelids sunken like there's nothing left in the sockets. The head stretched back, neck tendons standing out like wire. Mouth wide.

I can't move.

A girl's face, twisted in pain.

It looks dried out and mummified. Like it's been in there a long time.

My knees go weak and I stumble back. The throbbing of the pump pulses from the walls.

I stagger to the door and slam it behind me.

Run!

4

"STOP," DAD TELLS me. "Slow down and breathe. You're not making sense."

There was no one home when I rushed up to the apartment, so I had to track Dad down. He's replacing blown fuses on the fifteenth floor.

My heart is still hammering. Dad puts his hand on my shoulder to steady me, his face gone pale.

"You saw a body? In the basement?"

I nod, panting.

"A dead body? My God, where?"

"The incinerator room. Inside the wall. The old chute."

He frowns at me. "What do you mean? That's sealed up."

"There's a big hole in the wall. Must be from them tearing up the street. I saw cracks all around the door and went inside to check for more damage. That's when I found *it*."

"But that chute?" Dad is shaking his head. "It was emptied out before it was closed years ago."

"Are you hearing me? There's a girl's body stuffed inside."

I guess it finally hits him that I'm serious. He looks stunned.

"A girl?"

"Yeah. A teenager, maybe."

He's lost in shock for a long moment.

"Dad?"

"Yeah. I'll . . . I'll go check it out."

"Let me show you."

He shakes his head. "No. No, you wait in the apartment. Sit, calm down and catch your breath. I'll go look."

"But—"

"No buts. Just wait for me there. Don't do anything, just stay there till I come back."

We get on the elevator, and he lets me off on our floor before heading down alone. I go in the apartment and pace around the kitchen. Wherever I look I can't stop seeing that *thing*—it's scorched into the back of my eyes. Dried and mummified, preserved in death. Ripped open and gutted—

My stomach starts to heave. Rushing to the bathroom, I collapse on my knees and puke till I'm empty. My legs are so weak I have to pull myself up on the sink. I rinse my mouth and brush my teeth.

Then I sit on the edge of the tub till I can stand again. I go to my room and suck in deep breaths by the window, forehead pressed to the screen. Wish I could stick my head out into the sunlight, but Dad bolted screens onto all our windows, because Squirrel climbs on everything.

Standing here, I zone out for a while.

What's taking Dad so long? Is he calling the police? I don't see any cop cars. It's been maybe twenty minutes. Longer. What's he doing?

I try him on my cell, but it goes straight to voice mail.

That girl wasn't just killed, she was slaughtered. What kind of monster—

I jump at the sound of our apartment door opening. I find Dad in the kitchen, washing his hands in the sink.

"Dad?"

"Yeah." He keeps scrubbing, his back to me.

"So? You saw it? What do we do?"

He glances over, but it's like he's looking right through me, his eyes focused on something else. It takes a moment before his gaze locks on to mine.

"What?" he says.

"You saw it?"

Turning the water off, Dad dries his hands on a paper towel. "Honey, there was nothing but some old garbage in the chute. No body."

"What? You must have been looking in the wrong place. It's in the incinerator room, at the bottom of the chute. There's a huge crack in the wall. You can't miss it."

"I know where you mean, Tyne. But you're—you're wrong. It's dark in there, all shadows. Really, I—I dug around and there's just trash that got trapped and left behind when it was sealed shut."

"No. I saw it. That thing. It's a real dead body.

I had my flashlight and everything. Come on, I'll show you."

I move toward the door.

He just stands there, drying his hands. "Tyne, I believe you—that you think you saw something. But you must have been seeing things. I'm thinking maybe it's a side effect from the painkillers. They can mess with your brain, right? Make you see things. Hallucinate stuff."

"I wasn't hallucinating. I'm sure. I saw it."

"Just sit down for a minute."

"I can't sit. Let's go back down. You'll see."

"I was just there. And looked all around in the chute and the shaft."

He's not hearing me. "Whatever. I'll go myself. And take a picture of it for you." I wave my cell phone and head for the door.

Dad grabs my wrist. "Hold on. Just wait."

"For what?"

I can see him thinking that I'm freaking out. But he looks kind of shaken too. Maybe scared I'm losing it.

"Okay." He gives in. "But . . . calm down. You'll see it's nothing."

So we go. It's a long, quiet ride down on the elevator, till I break the silence.

"I'm not crazy."

"I wasn't saying that. It's just—you have to trust me on this."

We get off at the basement and the first thing I notice is the silence. That drumbeat pulse is gone.

"The pump?" I ask.

"Off. The flood's been drained."

As we approach the incinerator room, a cold sweat trickles icy fingers down the back of my neck. Dad steps over the rubble of fallen plaster and unlocks the door. It's still jammed, so he shoves it open.

My heart is hammering so hard it hurts.

Dad turns on his flashlight, a big one with a bright high beam that pushes the shadows back. I flick mine on too and follow him in.

"Over there," I whisper.

"I know." His deep voice echoes in here.

His boots kick up a haze of dust crossing the room. Dad stops in front of the gaping hole in the wall, and I have to force myself those last steps to join him. The rotten smell is very faint now, barely there. He shines his light into the chute. Glancing at him for his reaction before I lean in to look, all I see is his worried frown. Then I follow his light, bracing myself for that corpse. And—

It's not there. What the hell?

"It was here. I swear it."

Twisting around, I sweep my beam along the bottom, then up the shadowy tunnel of the shaft. As if that thing might be clinging to the sides up there or something, hiding. There's just a scattering of trash at the bottom, not enough to bury a body in.

"I don't . . . I don't understand. Can you smell that?"

He shrugs. "Might be a dead mouse. That's all."

I shake my head. "No. There was a body. I'm sure, really. . . ." I trail off.

Dad rests his hand on my arm. "Don't worry. Your painkillers are strong drugs; they can make you see things, especially in the dark. Hard to see anything in here."

"I don't know. Don't know."

"Let it go, Tyne. Come on, we'll get out of here. You get some fresh air and sunshine. This will all seem like a dream in no time."

I'm not sure what to do, what to think. But I follow him, lighting up the corners of the room as we go, searching for anything. To make sure nobody else was here between when I ran out and Dad came down to check, I study our shoe prints in the decades-old dust on the floor, and see that there are only mine and his. No tracks but ours.

And no sign of that thing crawling out of there and away on its own—which is crazy, I know.

I just want out. Now.

5

STEPPING OUT INTO the sunlight with Stick, my mind's a mess. Was I really hallucinating on my meds?

Stick puts his arm around my waist. As we walk down the block, I let him distract me.

Stick's a little bit of everything. He's got a mix of Latino-Caribbean and white blood that gives him mocha skin and crazy spiky curls that spring out in all directions. He has these electric-blue eyes, and it feels like there's a live current charging through him. It's contagious—his energy grabs me now.

Hard to say when me and Stick became a *thing*. I've known him since we were little and he moved into the Zoo. He's a foster kid who got bounced around a lot of homes before getting placed with a family here.

I met him in first grade. They always made me sit in the back of the class because I was so tall and blocked the view for the other kids. Stick stumbled in before the start of class one morning, and went up to the teacher's desk with a note and his goofy smile.

She told him to take one of the empty desks in back. When he caught sight of me he waved like we were old friends, sat next to me and started talking non-stop.

"Hey, I saw you at my new building. So we're neighbors there, and we're neighbors here too in class, I guess. I'm the new guy. I'm always the new guy, everywhere I go. I'm a foster kid and I move around a lot. I make a map when they send me to a new place so I know where I am and where to go home. The map's got my new address and phone number on it, my new mom's name and everything."

He pulled out his map. It showed our neighborhood, with the streets and our school marked on it.

"My sister—not my real sister, she's a foster too but older—she'll take me home after school. My name is Ricky, but my new sister calls me Stick. We share a room, and she says if I touch her stuff she'll snap me like a stick. She calls me that so I won't forget, and because I'm skinny like a stick. You can call me that too if you want. I get new numbers and everything, so I guess I get a new name too."

He was breathless at the end, wheezing. I just sat there, stunned that anybody could say so much so fast.

Since then he's always been there, following me around like a lost puppy at the start, then as my side-kick exploring the city, and somewhere in these past few years he became my guy. At first it felt weird, but now it's so right—as we walk down the street, his hand on my hip feels like it belongs there.

"—like a grave," he's saying.

I don't catch the rest. I hear "grave" and it's like he's reading my mind as I flash back to the vision of the body in the wall.

"What? What's like a grave?"

"This." Stick waves his hand at the block-long trench where our street used to be, dug up to replace the sewer lines. "A grave big enough for a giant. Like you." He laughs. "Hey, I was thinking we gotta get you a new nickname for when you're playing hoops. I mean, some of the ones you've got are okay—Girlzilla, Titanic—but you want something real catchy for when you go pro."

"What are you talking about? Pro? I'll be lucky if I can score a college scholarship."

Stick's always dreaming.

"Hear me out," he says. "I was thinking of something like *Amazon,* after those legendary girl warriors. But how about—*Slamazon.* For when you slam-dunk. *Slam-dunk-damn-azon.*"

"You don't get to choose your nickname," I tell him. "You get stuck with whatever sticks to you. Like *Stick*!"

And besides, slam-dunking is what got me hurt and sidelined for the past three weeks. We were playing against Rawlings, a private school, and we were up by ten points late in the game. All we had to do was run out the clock. But they were the rich kids and we were the public school bottom-feeders, so we had to show them up on their home court.

My girls were pushing me to try a move I'd only made in practice, and slam dunk. Dunking is really rare in girls' basketball, where most of us don't have the height or jump to make the move like the guys. But that night I was feeling lucky, and when I got an open run at the basket I went for it. I had the speed, the jump and elevation perfect—the whole calculus. I went airborne, flying to the hoop and slamming it. But what goes up must come down. While my team went wild at the shot, I landed off-balance where the court was slippery with sweat, my right leg buckled, hyperextending my knee and damaging my MCL.

I've rerun that moment a million times since, wishing I could replay it any other way. Lying there on the court in a world of pain, my life didn't flash in front of my eyes, but my future did. Because basketball is my only escape from the Zoo. No way I want to inherit the family business, being super like Dad and his dad before him. This girl's got to go!

"You're not limping so bad," Stick says.

"Yeah, and the doc told me I don't have to wear the knee brace all the time now."

"Is it still hurting?"

"Not so much when I get it warmed up and moving. And the pills take the edge off."

But what else are the pills doing to me?

"Any time you need a massage, I'm there." His hand slips from my waist to rub the small of my back. "You know my magic fingers."

"Your magic massages always wander higher than my knee."

He waggles his eyebrows at me. "I'm a full-service body mechanic."

I can't help cracking up. I'm glad Stick sees the girl behind the giant; nobody else does. If I wear a lot of makeup, I look ridiculous. My wardrobe of T-shirts, hoodies and track pants comes from the men's department. It's the only stuff that fits. In a dress or a skirt, with my broad shoulders and slim hips, I come off like a drag queen.

We pass by the homeless shelter on the end of the street.

Our block, with its towering Zoo, is like an island of slum in downtown Toronto. The last ruins of the old ghetto that used to dominate the area. On the edge of what they call Cabbagetown, which got its name back when it was home to the poorest of the poor who couldn't waste any space on lawns, so they grew cabbages in their yards instead of grass. Now the area is full of new condos and swanky stores. The Zoo is all that's left; we're castaways surrounded by an ocean of urban redevelopment.

"Where we headed?" I ask.

"Paradise."

Pizza Paradise has a dim, smoky interior lit by the oven fire in back. The place is a grease pit, with earsplitting metal music and a dark vibe that scares off most people. It should say *eat at your own risk,* but they've got the cheapest pies in town, and they're death-defyingly yummy.

"So, you buying?" Stick asks, flashing his goofy grin. The guy's always broke.

"Sure, I just got paid."

Dad gave me extra—disaster pay.

"Save us a spot," Stick says, grabbing some cash and diving inside.

I sit on the bench out front, stretching my knee. Another week and I'll be back in practice.

I came late to basketball. Never was a jock, couldn't keep up with my body as it grew so big, so fast. Always awkward and out of control. When you see me coming, you think: that girl was made to play hoops. But when you grow up being stared at, laughed at and yelled at in the street—slammed for my size—the last thing you want is to get in front of a crowd and make yourself an easy target. Then, last year, I realized my grades weren't going to win a scholarship and basketball might be my ticket out. So I went to Dad and said show me the game.

He played in high school, but his game days ended when he snapped an Achilles tendon. He still walks with a hitch in his step. That's why he never pushed hoops on me. He didn't want his girl limping through life like him.

When I play it ain't pretty. I run around the court like Godzilla trashing Tokyo. You try dancing with size fourteen feet. But a funny thing happened when I got into the game—nobody was laughing at me anymore; they were cheering. And I was hooked. I like being where my size matters.

The noon sun chases away the December chill,

warming me. And the creeps are starting to fade. Like Dad said, it was a pharmaceutical hallucination. I checked, and that's a possible side effect of the pills.

But it seemed so real, the sight of it, and the *feel* of being close-up with death, like nothing else. How could my brain fake all that?

Stick comes out of the Paradise smoke cloud with two larges and slides down beside me on the bench.

"I'm not that hungry," I say as he flips the boxes open to reveal the pizzas in all their greasy glory.

"Who says you're getting any?"

Stick's got a huge appetite and a nuclear metabolism that burns it all off. The pies are delicious. What exactly the meats are on our 3 Meat pizzas is a mystery, and there's enough cheese to give you a heart attack—but what a way to go.

"We should practice shooting free throws, Tyne. Don't want you losing your touch."

"What touch? I'm no shooter."

My role on the team is shot blocking, rebounding, smackdown defensive demon. I muscle girls out of the way. Stick helps me practice, but him guarding me is like setting a Chihuahua on a Great Dane. With Dad it's more of a fair fight.

Thinking of him now, I see his face in the beam of my flashlight down in the dark by the hole in the wall. *It'll seem like a dream.* But it's still so fresh in my head that I drop my slice back in the box.

"What's up? You sick or something? I've been getting a weird vibe off you today."

"Can I tell you something crazy?"

"Sure. I'm into crazy."

So I start with the flood, and the crack in the wall. I describe the body, how it looked all dried up and mummified.

I keep my eyes off Stick while I'm talking, not wanting to see the same disbelief I got from Dad. After I'm done with how the body was gone when we returned, I let the silence stretch out, waiting for Stick to break it.

"For real?" he asks.

I nod, meeting his gaze. I see questions there, but he's not looking at me like I'm nuts.

"So?" I say. "What do you think?"

"Well, I was thinking of fun in the sun. But this beats that." He gets up from the bench. "Show me. Take me to the *tomb*."

6

DARKNESS AND DUST.

But no body.

I shine the beam of the big flashlight into the hole, with Stick leaning in close. Only there's nothing to see.

"It was here."

He steps back and looks around the empty room. "So where did it go?"

I changed the bulb so we wouldn't be stumbling around in the dark. But something about this place drains the light.

"Let's check in there," Stick says, going over to the huge smoke-blackened door of the incinerator on the far wall.

"Why? That thing I saw didn't get out of the wall to go hide in there."

"Look at the size of that furnace." He snaps a shot of it with his phone. "You could stuff a bunch of bodies inside. Come on, let's just check and see. Open it up."

"You do it."

"No way. You're the super's daughter. You've got the master key."

I check the latch on the incinerator. "It's not locked."

"Crack it open. If some undead freak jumps out, I've got your back." Stick picks up the garbage shovel leaning against the wall and holds it, ready to swing.

"You're my hero." I shake my head. This is pointless, but now he's got me wondering what might be inside.

Grabbing the cold metal latch, I strain to move it. But the thing is stuck like it's welded shut.

"Won't budge," I say. "Try hitting it with the shovel."

Stick whacks it hard twice with clanging booms. "That'll wake the dead."

Gripping the latch again, I twist till it gives with a screech, breaking loose a seal of rust. Opening the door wide, I aim the flashlight into the depths of the furnace.

Ash and charcoal are heaped two feet deep inside. No bones or body parts.

"Shovel around in there," I tell him.

Just some old cans and bottle caps show up. If there was ever a body in there, it's long gone to ash. A smoky dust cloud wafts out.

"Enough." I cough, waving the dust away as I swing the door shut with a thud.

"Now what?" Stick leans on the shovel.

I go back to that hole. The crack runs from the ceiling halfway to the floor. I can peer in, but I can't reach the shallow layer of trash on the bottom. It's not deep enough to hide anything. The body's gone. But maybe there's something in there. The gap is a little more than a foot wide. Too tight for me. Maybe big enough for Stick to fit through. The shaft inside is a bit wider here in the basement where the chute emptied out.

"Think you could get in there?"

"What? Why?"

"To get a closer look at that crap. See if there's some kind of . . . I don't know, *something*. Proof of what I saw."

"You want me to climb in a hole in the wall where you think you saw a corpse and dig through garbage?"

I nod.

"Worst date ever."

"Hey, I bought you lunch."

"How about I pay you back with something more stimulating," he says, trying his best sexy, smoldering look on me.

"Maybe later. This place isn't putting me in the mood." I stick my head in the gap, running the light over the pile of debris. "Come on, I need to know if anything's buried under that."

"Why don't you do it?"

"I couldn't fit one leg in there. So get your cute little butt in."

He sighs. "Anything for my girl."

"Here. Use these to dig." I pull some latex gloves from my tool kit. "No room for the shovel in there."

I drag the abandoned chair over to help Stick climb through. He gets on it, swings one leg into the gap, then squirms and squeezes inside, landing with a crunch in the trash. I give him the flashlight, and he sweeps the beam over the walls of the shaft and up into the impenetrable blackness of the chute.

"Creepy," he says. "If something drags me off in the dark for its next meal, I will come back to haunt you."

"You already haunt me."

He starts kicking around in the garbage. "So what am I supposed to be looking for, anyway?"

"I don't know. Anything suspicious, or weird."

"We're way past weird here. You know, there are professors who study old trash. They're called garbologists. Saw a show on TV about them. They go digging up landfills and dumps to see how people lived centuries ago. They say a lot of archaeology is just digging through crap our ancestors threw out."

"Finding anything, Professor Stick?"

With no room to bend over, he has to squat to pick something up.

"How's this for weird?"

He hands me a filthy stuffed toy. It's Ernie from *Sesame Street,* with one eye ripped off, his head hanging on by a thread and his stuffing spilling out.

"You think Bert did that to him?" Stick says. "He was always screaming at Ernie to shut up at bedtime. Maybe he pushed Ernie down the chute."

"Well, Bert did have anger management issues,

and that sinister unibrow. But I don't think this Muppet murder is connected to what I saw."

I set the toy down. Stick spends another few minutes sorting through the debris, joking about starring in *Indiana Jones and the Slum Mummy's Tomb.*

Then he freezes.

"You got something?"

"I don't know." Rising from a crouch, he shines the light on what he's holding.

Looks like a gray twig, about three inches long. Or maybe a broken pencil.

"Tell me that's not what I think it is," he says.

I take it, turning it over in the glare of the beam.

My breath catches, and my guts go ice cold.

It's a finger.

7

I CAN'T BELIEVE it.

Sitting at my desk in my room, deep in the night, I stare at the finger, a dry, brittle and shriveled gray thing. I've got it in a clear plastic pill bottle.

It's real. I keep staring as if it's going to disappear like the rest of the body. After making the grisly discovery, we did a thorough search, with Stick dumping everything out to be examined in the light, but there was nothing else.

Where's the rest of you?

Now there's no doubt that everything I saw was real. But what happened to the corpse between when I found it and when I went back down with Dad?

That's what's killing me. Because I'm sure there were only two sets of shoe prints in the old dust on the floor—mine and his. Nobody else had been there. That door was locked tight.

It's insane. But there's no way around it: Dad must have moved the body. Then he lied to me and tried to make me think I was seeing things.

But that's crazy! Makes no sense. Why would he do that?

I've been hiding out in my room, skipping the spaghetti Mom made before heading to work. I said I ate earlier.

I can't face Dad. He made me think I was nuts.

I replay it all: how nervous he seemed when he came back up from the basement to tell me there was nothing in the chute, how he kept washing his hands and wouldn't look at me.

Is it possible?

Where did he put the body? He was gone maybe twenty minutes. Not enough time to take the corpse off the property. It might still be down there.

The basement floors of the Zoo have so many hiding places, utility and storage rooms, supply closets, crawl spaces and forgotten compartments. It's a maze of twisting hallways, some ending in brick walls as if the builders were just making things up as they went along. If Dad hid something, I'd never find it.

Stick was as shocked as me, but fascinated too. We've been talking and texting all night. On my laptop screen right now is one of the links he sent me, to a site that tells you all about "natural" mummification. That's where, under the right conditions, a dead body will dry out and stay in a "preserved" state. I'm getting the shakes just thinking about it.

Hard to tell from what I saw, but she was young. A teenager, maybe. A girl, like me. The thought pierces my heart.

Holding the bottle under my desk lamp, I study the finger. We noticed some old scarring on the skin where a ring would go. Some kind of design, what looks like a little skull, with some letters. It's hard to make out.

What do I do with this? Can't take it to the cops—not if Dad's concealing the rest of the body. Who does that? It's not how an innocent man acts. But there's no way he could ever be involved in anything like this.

Impossible. Unbelievable.

But I'm holding the proof that he's lying.

So I lock myself in my room, away from Dad, who's suddenly a stranger to me.

I look at the finger, seeing nightmare flashes of the girl in the wall. That poor thing.

Who were you? How did you die? And why is he hiding you?

8

"NO WAY," STICK says. "My brain just can't go there."

We're at his apartment on Sunday morning. I sneaked out early before Dad got up. I'm on Stick's couch, exhausted after a sleepless night.

"There's got to be some innocent explanation," he says.

"Give me one."

He can only shake his head.

"Exactly. Believe me, I broke my brain trying to come up with one."

This is where Stick lives with his foster family. A lot of kids have come and gone from this place—some were sent here by the court while their parents were jailed or in rehab; others were abuse victims removed from their homes or abandoned kids who were given up to the state, like Stick. Most were temporary, till they got sent back to their real families; others left when they got adopted. Then there's Stick—he's a lifer. The place is run by Miss Diaz, mom to a mob of stray kids over the years.

"Come on," Stick says. "This is your dad we're talking about. Teddy. Everybody calls him Teddy Bear because he's always helping people, looking out for everybody. Letting them pay the rent late sometimes. Fixing stuff, even when it's not his job—you know, like vacuum cleaners, air conditioners and bikes. Checking in on the old folks. When I fell off the jungle gym in the park and dislocated my shoulder, remember how he popped it back in place, then got me to the hospital and later bought me all the ice cream I could eat? He'd never do something like this. You know him."

"Yeah, well, I thought I did."

Dad's the closest thing to a father figure Stick's ever had. I've even heard Dad call him *son* a few times, just being casual, but I could see how Stick felt it.

"What if you just confront him? I mean, show him that finger and say 'Here's the proof. I saw what I saw.' "

"Yeah, and then what? I say, 'By the way, Daddy, what did you do with the body?' Believe me, I imagined the scene a million times last night. How it would go. But what could he say? What possible innocent reason could there be? There's nothing. And he's already lied about it. Told me I was crazy, seeing things, hallucinating. I can't take him lying to me again."

"But you've got evidence. How could he deny it?"

I've thought about that too. "Lots of ways. He could say the finger's not real. Like it's a Halloween prop, made to look like the real thing, that somebody threw out. Or it's from something else—a monkey or something.

41

The way it looks, it's hard to tell. Or he might even say it's from some old construction accident."

"That's kind of far-fetched."

"Doesn't matter. He could say anything to talk his way out of it, like he did yesterday. Make enough room for doubt. But I know what's real. That finger—that body—is real. And I can't take any more lies."

Dad trying to trick me—that's one hell of a head fake.

We sit silent for a minute. Stick grabs a Pop-Tart from the box on the coffee table where I've got my leg up, resting my sore knee. Nothing keeps him from eating. Not even the photo of the finger, which he brings up on his cell phone.

"You know," he says, "the cops could pull a print off it. And if she was ever in the system they could ID her."

"Can't go to the cops."

"I know. I'm just saying."

"What about that design?" I ask. "The scarring? What do you think?"

"I might have something on that. You're not the only one who went sleepless last night. I was searching online and I think I know what it is. See the way the scar is raised?"

Before I sealed the finger in the bottle, we gave the thing a thorough inspection, feeling the bumps of those lines under our fingertips.

"That wasn't cut into the skin. It was burned into it. Branded."

"What?"

"Yeah, it's called a ring brand. Some people get them instead of tattoos. You get stamped by a hot metal brand with some design, and it leaves this kind of scar. Here, check these out."

He flips through shots he got off Google of different brands done on shoulders, biceps, necks and fingers, ending with a close-up of the finger's markings.

"I played with the contrast on the photo to make the pattern clearer, and I came up with this."

The outline of the little skull pops out. The design is only the top half of a skull. There's something else in the place where the teeth and jaws would be.

"What is that?" I say. "Looks like a flower."

"Yeah."

"What's it supposed to mean?"

"No idea. Possibly a gang thing? I'll check around some sites and see if I can find a match."

"What about the letters on the other side?"

Stick brings up a shot of the palm-side of the finger, with the tiny, hard-to-read letters now standing out pale and clear:

MIVEM

"What's MIVEM?" I ask.

"Maybe her name?"

I grunt. "Who gets branded with their name?"

"Who does any of this, gets white-hot metal burned into their flesh?"

"She did. So it must have meant something to her."

"Could be anything. A message. Some personal code."

There's something vaguely familiar about the little flowering skull, like maybe I've seen something like it before. But the feeling is so faint that I might be imagining it.

As I'm trying to puzzle out those letters, the bedroom door opens and out comes Stick's foster sister, Vega, in a camouflage T-shirt and boxers.

She squints at us, just woken up. Vega is half black, half Asian—a *blazin,* she calls herself. It fits—she's on fire. She's lean and muscled, with hair in ragged cornrows that stick up like barbed wire.

"Morning, bitches." Vega goes in the kitchen, grabs a can of Red Bull and chugs it. "Breakfast of champions." She belches thunderously.

"Hey, Stick," she calls, tapping a sheet of paper magneted to the fridge. "This chore chart here isn't just for decoration. And it's saying clean the bathroom, like, yesterday. So you better be getting in there and scrubbing that tub. You know Miss Diaz needs a hot soak for her arthritis."

"I'm getting to it."

"Make sure you get to it before she comes home from church."

Vega has always been the enforcer. Miss D is too old to chase kids around anymore, so Vega lays down the law. Which sounds funny, considering her criminal record. It's impressive, ending with a two-month sentence in juvie, for breaking into cars and stealing stereos and consoles. She used to brag she could get in and get gone before anybody even heard the car alarm—stealing at the speed of sound.

But Vega's been clean for over a year now, after Miss D gave her a final ultimatum—*get legal or get gone*. Now she's in the Jail to Jobs program, working as a mechanic at a local garage. Fixing what she used to break.

She grabs a Pop-Tart. "How's the knee, Stretch? We gonna see you back on the court soon?"

"Two more weeks. It was only a partial tear, didn't need surgery. But it's bad enough."

"Yeah? Well, check this out." Vega leans over to show me a jagged scar on her forearm. "Compound fracture when I was ten. Bone broke through the skin. It scared the crap out of my stepdad after he did that. He thought they were going to jail his ass. But he got off."

"Tell her the punch line to the story," Stick says.

"Oh. A week later, Stepdick got some antifreeze mixed in with his beer. He wasn't up for beatdowns after that."

Crazy stuff, but not so shocking coming from Vega. I can see her as a ten-year-old poisoner.

"Ah, memories," she says, heading toward the bathroom. "Anyway, I'm hitting the shower. Then you can scrub the tub, Stick."

Hard to believe she's only two years older than us. She's actually aged out of the foster system, but she still lives here with Miss Diaz. You don't want to get on Vega's bad side. But in her own way she's been a badass big sister to Stick.

Back after Stick took a beating from the class bully, Caveman Connor, Vega tried toughening Stick up, showing him some moves.

He was safe whenever I was around. Nobody tried anything with me towering beside him to back him up.

But like Vega said, "Stretch can't always be there to save you. She ain't your bodyguard."

The problem was Stick had toothpick arms and twiggy legs—no power. So Vega had nothing to work with trying to train him.

"You've got zero muscle," she told him. "But a huge head. You're like a walking lollipop. So that'll be your weapon."

Then she taught him how to head butt, making him practice on a stuffed Mickey Mouse doll.

"That other kid's nothing but a big fat mouse," she said. "But you and me, Stick, we're ghetto rats. You've seen those things—born mean, with needle teeth and razor claws. If they don't start fighting first thing, they get eaten. That's what you are, a baby rat."

He nodded, looking about as mean as a fuzzy puppy.

"Don't waste time on punching and kicking, just get in close. You gotta jump him and hold on tight. Then, bang!" Vega knocked heads with the stuffed toy, demonstrating how to pull your head back before whipping it forward and making contact. She explained how to do the most damage without knocking yourself out at the same time, instructing Stick on angles of impact and where his own skull was thickest.

"Right here." She tapped his forehead. "Aim with that. If you're coming in low, you can catch him under the chin. That'll stun him. Crack him on the nose and you'll get him bleeding. If he slips around behind you, snap back and try to catch him in the teeth."

She got Stick wrestling Mickey and practicing till he was breathless and dizzy.

"Banging heads," he said. "Won't that hurt my brain?"

"What brain? Just knock that fat mouse out."

And so, the next day at lunch in the school cafeteria, when Vega spotted Connor heading to the washroom, she told Stick to go for it. "Now's your chance."

"I hide from him. I don't go *looking* for him."

"Be the hunter, not the hunted. Surprise is a weapon too."

So me and Vega followed Stick as he trailed Connor to the boys' room. There were a few guys in there, which meant an audience. Vega gave Stick a shove.

"Do it!"

Connor was turning to see what was going on when Stick crashed into him, and half hugged, half tackled the bigger kid. It was a short, messy fight, with the other kids looking on in shock, some cheering for Stick. The Caveman got a few shots in, trying to break Stick's hold, and our boy hanging on tight. Stick's first head butt caught Connor on the temple, knocking him off-balance. Then Stick hammered the top of his skull up under Connor's chin. They both went down, rolling on the floor. Somebody started crying, and there was a lot of blood. Connor had bitten his tongue when their heads smacked, and he was gushing. I went over to Stick, who was sitting stunned on the tiles, blinking dizzy and dazed up at me.

"Wow," he kept saying. "Wow." He tried to stand up, but his legs were all rubbery and he tumbled to his knees. "What happened?"

Vega was shaking her head, but with the ghost of a smile. "Get him up, Stretch."

Connor left him alone after that, but Vega never did toughen Stick. While she was a rat, he was always going to be more of a hamster.

"When?" he asks me now.

"Huh?" I didn't catch the rest of what he just said. "When what?"

"When was the incinerator chute sealed up? If we know that, it'll give us an idea when the girl was dumped in there, right? Some kind of range for when she died."

"It's been shut like that for as long as I can remember."

"But can you find out how long?"

I think; then it hits me. "The logbook."

"What's that?"

"We have to keep records of all repairs and renovations done in the building. City regulations."

"So you can check when the shaft was patched up?"

"The old logs are down in storage. I could dig them up. That might give us a timeline."

And it could give us more. Because those books don't just show what jobs were done. They show who did the work.

Who buried her in the wall.

9

NOBODY COMES HERE. This section of the basement is locked off, and you need the master key to get this far. Not that there's anything dangerous or forbidden. It's just claustrophobic corridors and empty rooms, like some kind of bunker or nuclear fallout shelter that we've never had any use for.

When me and Stick were kids I'd steal the key and we'd dare each other to race through the maze, where one wrong turn could get you lost and never heard from again.

I used to follow Dad everywhere when I was little. He took me down here, and I thought this section, with its long hallways of shut doors, was the building's jail, where the bad tenants got locked up for not paying rent, playing music too loud or fighting with their neighbors. I remember holding on to Dad's belt the whole time we were here, in case one of those prisoners reached out from a dark cell and dragged me in.

The sound of my steps breaks the deep silence. In

the long stretches between lights, pools of shadows gather. At the end of a hallway I stop to listen. Was that the echo of my own steps? Or something else? I strain my ears.

Getting jumpy, that's all. I'm alone here. I'm sure.

Turning a corner, I come to storage room 33. My hand shakes slightly as I unlock the door.

A breath of stale air wafts out as I reach in and find the switch. In the light from a single low-watt bulb I see stacks of boxes and a beat-up table and chair. All the Zoo's old records are in cardboard boxes labeled with marker. Invoices, forms and reports, decades of paperwork and long tubes that hold blueprints for electrical and plumbing layouts. And the logs.

I know the incinerator was shut down before I was born, back when Toronto was known as the Big Smoke because of its smog. The garbage chute must have been sealed up around then too. So I decide to work my way back, starting with the year of my birth. I grab a box that covers the decade leading up to when I was born, and sit at the table.

The log is crammed with notations, documenting an apocalypse of floods and fires, plagues of mice and roaches, bedbugs, toxic molds. Boiler breakdowns, dead appliances, accidental electrocutions from faulty wiring, plumbing problems and shattered windows. The logs list the repairs and who did the fixing.

As I go through the years, I find Dad's initials beside the jobs: *TG* for Ted Greer. He's been superintendent since he took over from his own father, who died when Dad was in high school. Dad got stuck with the job because he had to help support the family and take care of his mother.

Dad's older brother Jake's initials are nowhere to be found. Uncle Jake likes to say the janitor gene skipped him. Jake escaped and started his own construction company. He's got a huge house out in the suburbs.

There's no reference to the incinerator. I finish up one box of logs and take another down. A different set of initials begins to appear, mixed in with Dad's. *DG,* his father, Douglas. Dad was helping out long before he became super.

Now I'm the helper. Dad says we make a great team, calls me a natural problem solver.

After my sleepless night, the writing is starting to blur together when I finally spot something. *Incinerator shut down. Gas line blocked.*

The date is eight years before I was born, when Dad would have been fourteen. The initials beside the note are *DG.*

Searching further, I find this: *Incinerator drawers removed. Floors 15–25. Walls plastered. DG.*

In the following week, the drawers for the lower floors are removed. Different dates, same *DG* next to them.

I flip pages. Where is it? Come on.

There! Six months later: *Incinerator room. Chute drywalled shut.* But no initials. Nothing to indicate who did that final job, sealing in the body. I try comparing the handwriting with the earlier notes, but it's all scribbles. Can't tell if it's the same.

But *DG* did the rest of the work.

I sit back and rub my face. Did he put her in there? Did she know him, my grandfather? Did he do it?

I check the dates again. Why so long between when the walls were patched on the floors above and the sealing up of the chute in the basement? Maybe there was no rush because nobody could toss any trash down the shaft with the drawers plastered over. And they got distracted by the constant repairs. So it could wait, that final closing of the chute.

Or maybe there was no rush till there was a body to hide.

10

HERE'S WHERE I go to get away from everything. To breathe.

The roof is off-limits. But I've got the key to the kingdom. It's quieter twenty-six stories up, high above the traffic and wrecking crews. The air seems a little cleaner, and I don't have to worry about fitting into the world. No ceiling to crowd me. Nothing but sky.

Me and Stick sneak up here to be alone, so we don't have to worry about anybody busting in on us. We roll out yoga mats to make a love nest between the tall ventilation fans where we can be together, hidden and safe from snooping eyes.

I keep lawn chairs up here too. I drag one over for the best view. Down the corridor of skyscrapers I can catch a peek at Lake Ontario, and the sailboats drifting by.

I sit and try to make sense of this mess.

If it was Dad's father who sealed up the chute, he must be the one who dumped the body inside.

Stuffed her in that garbage bag like trash and hid her in the wall.

Who was my grandfather, anyway? I never knew him. He died before I was born—died young, from a stroke. But everything I've ever heard about him is ugly and awful.

When we were all out at my uncle Jake's house for Thanksgiving a few years back, Dad's big brother started talking about the bad old days, living in the shadow of their old man.

Me, Dad and Jake were down in the basement, playing a game of snooker on the pool table. Jake was about six beers deep by then. Not raving drunk, but getting there.

"Like growing up in a minefield," he said to me as he lined up a shot. "You never knew when your next step might set the old man off. And when he went off, he went way off." Missing his shot, Jake leaned in close, breathing beer fumes on me as Dad frowned at him. "They called him Mad Dog. Mad Dog Doug. Remember, Teddy, how his face would go all red? Like he was going to blow."

Dad tried to cut him off. "She doesn't need to hear this."

But Jake was picking up speed. "And there was nowhere to hide in that little rathole apartment. Don't know why you're still living there, brother. Come work for me. Get you out of the Zoo."

"I've got a job."

"That's not a job. It's a curse," Jake said, waving

his pool stick around. "Anyway, you couldn't escape old Mad Dog. You were his favorite punching bag, Teddy. He hated you best. Hated you for being so big, when he was so small—five and a half feet of mean and vicious. Hated you for getting in the way when he went after Mom, and taking it for her." Jake gave me a drunken grin. "Kid, your dad really knew how to take a beating."

"Shut up, Jake." Dad pulled me away, taking my stick and setting it on the table.

"What, am I wrong? We all got a taste of his fists, but you were his favorite. And you never fought back, never threw a punch. You're a giant, brother. Could have squashed him like a bug if you tried."

Dad was leading me upstairs when Jake called out something that's stuck in my head ever since. "But you got him back in the end, didn't you, Teddy? Beat Mad Dog without laying a hand on him. You got the last laugh."

Dad kept me away from Uncle Jake for the rest of that Thanksgiving. Later, when I asked him what that final remark meant, Dad said, "Ancient history. Forget it."

All I know for sure is my grandfather smacked them all around, even my grandmother. She lives with Jake and his wife now.

Gran's a shy, gray lady who barely talks above a whisper. She used to have a little garden up here on the roof, and there are still a few broken pots and planters lying around.

So, Mad Dog was an abuser. Still, it's a big step to murder. And what happened to the girl was the work of a psycho.

If Mad Dog was the killer, why would Dad be covering up now, after all these years? No excuse would be good enough, no explanation would make sense.

My gaze shifts across the rooftop to the incinerator chimney. If that furnace hadn't been shut down, the body probably would have been burned to ash, erased and forgotten.

For my whole life, that body was buried beneath me. Did Dad know it was there all this time? He seemed surprised when I came running to tell him what I had found.

But he's hiding it now. Keeping a secret.

It's like a shadow cast over my life, and over every minute with him.

Like it was all a lie. I never really knew Dad.

11

DAD'S OUT WHEN I come down from the roof. I poke my head in the kitchen and find Mom making lunch.

"Hey, Ty, where you been? I got up this morning and everybody was gone."

"I was just hanging with Stick."

"Hungry?"

I realize I'm starving. Been so obsessed I forgot to eat.

"I could eat a herd of horses," I say, before realizing that's one of Dad's lines that always made me giggle when I was little.

"How about a herd of grilled cheese sandwiches?"

"Triple cheese deluxe?"

"You grate, I'll grill."

The way we make the sandwiches is with a slice of good old rubbery processed cheese covered in shredded Monterey Jack and a thin shaving of chili pepper cheddar to give it a spicy kick.

I can hear Squirrel in the living room talking to

Animal Planet on the TV. Like it's a conversation and the people on the screen are talking back.

"Look out for the lion," he's saying. "It's sneaking up on you."

"Where's Dad?" I ask Mom.

"He left a note about picking up some plumbing parts. Been gone all morning."

I shred while she butters and stacks the slices. Between me, Mom and Squirrel we can eat half a dozen easy.

"Don't think he slept at all last night," Mom says.

What kept him up? What's he thinking? All I've got running through my head is, Why, why, why—

"Why what?" Mom startles me. I must have been thinking out loud, I'm so groggy and out of it.

"Why?" I try to make something up quick. "Why Dad? I mean . . . what was it about him? Why did you go for him, way back when?"

A good save, and a safe topic.

"I had my eye on Teddy, from around the block and school. You couldn't miss him. Whatever crowd he was in, he was above and beyond, head in the clouds. And he had his eye on me too. But who didn't, back then? All the guys were chasing me. They used to call me Red Hot, and not just because of my hair. Don't laugh, it's true. So anyway, you know your dad, he goes in slow motion. He was taking forever to make his move, so I told him to quit staring and ask me out already."

"So, just because he was big and tall you went for him?"

Mom flips the first sandwich on the frying pan with a buttery sizzle.

Squirrel is chattering in the other room: "Watch out. Lion's hiding in the grass."

"That's how he caught my eye. But he caught my heart with the way he was so much the opposite of me. I was out of control and out of my mind most of the time. And here he was so big and solid, something to hold on to. I'd lived fast before, had some fun. But what I really needed was how he slowed me down. He kept me from cracking up. Kept me sane."

She slides two grilled cheeses onto a plate for me and starts another.

"And your father always had that sexy, smoky voice."

I laugh. For me it's more of a comforting, deep bearlike rumble, but Mom calls it whiskey smoke, though Dad has never touched a drop or taken a puff.

"Plus, Teddy's got those great big hands."

I cough. "I'm trying to eat here."

She grins, enjoying scandalizing me.

Squirrel's yelling at his show. "Look out! Lion's coming. Run. Run!"

Mom nibbles on some shredded cheddar. "Back when I met Teddy, it was just me and my mother against the world. She kept losing jobs, and we moved around so much we stopped unpacking and just lived out of our suitcases. Riding the eviction express, she called it. Wasn't her fault, just a run of bad luck and bad guys. Our last stop was a roachy little apartment down the block from here in the Weeds."

That dump got torn down years ago.

"My mom worked two jobs. When I ran into your dad, being around him gave me this new feeling, one I'd never felt before. Made me feel like there was a place for me in the world—beside him. He felt like . . . *home*."

She leans her hip on the counter, watching me eat, smiling about something.

"What?" I say.

"You're so much like him. On the outside and inside."

I just look at her. I'm not even sure who Dad is anymore.

"Ever catch him in a lie?" I ask.

She frowns. "Teddy Bear? He couldn't lie to save his life."

Right. Maybe I'm not the only one who doesn't really know him.

"He's lousy at it," Mom goes on. "He has too many tells that give him away whenever he tries to stretch the truth. You know, the way he won't meet your eyes, or keeps trying to clear his throat like there's something caught in there. And he'll start twisting his ring like it's itching his finger. I always know."

When he told me I was seeing things, he was looking everywhere but at me, and coughing like he was choking on his lie.

Squirrel shows up now. "Dumb zebra. I warned him. Now he's lunch." He sniffs the cheesy air. "Lunch?"

Mom flips a sandwich onto a plate for him.

"You know they can't hear you," I tell him. "The TV animals and people."

"They hear me. For sure. Sometimes they talk back."

"He's nuts, Mom. Our mad munchkin." I reach down to pat the fiery red hair he got from her.

"Mad munching." Squirrel smiles, pulling apart his sandwich.

Mom pours him some apple juice. "He's only eight. Crazy in a good way, where he believes in everything. Infinite possibilities. Let him have his magic."

He believes in everything. What do I still believe in? What can I trust?

I'm eating my second sandwich when I hear the front door open. Dad's home.

I make a quick exit to my room, and text Stick: Got some new weirdness to share.

He comes back with: Done with chores. Let's make a jailbreak.

I slip out of my room and lock the door. Don't want a snooping Squirrel finding the finger I've hidden. I sneak down the hall, avoiding the kitchen, where Dad's doing his growly bear voice.

"I eat squirrels for breakfast!" he says, to squeals of laughter from Squirrel.

At the front door I bend to pull on my sneakers and notice Dad's work boots on the shoe mat. They're covered in fresh mud.

That stops me. We've had a long dry spell. It hasn't rained in over a month, and no snow yet. And downtown Toronto is like a concrete desert anyway.

But these boots were sunk ankle-deep in some serious muck today, while Dad was supposed to be out getting plumbing parts. I crouch down and turn one over to find dark damp earth caked in the treads.

Where did that come from?

Where was he really? And what was he doing?

12

"WHAT'S GOING ON?" Stick asks as I shut the door to the office behind us.

The manager's office in the lobby is where Dad does stuff like collecting rent checks, processing applications for new tenants, and taking complaints.

"I need to check on something," I say.

The room has a big desk with a laptop, lots of filing cabinets and a wall covered in notices about rules and regulations, city bylaws and tenant rights. Everything's neat and tidy, the way Dad likes it.

Two video monitors that show views of the building entrances are mounted on the wall facing the desk.

"There." I point at the screens.

"What's this gotta do with some muddy boots?"

I go behind the desk and turn on the computer. "Maybe nothing. Maybe everything."

After accessing the program for the security cameras, I search through the files. I've seen Dad do this to get footage whenever the mailboxes are broken into.

I pull up the memory files. "These monitors cover the front and back entrances."

"How about the cameras on the elevators?" Stick asks. "And the ones in the laundry room, and the lockers?"

"They don't work, just dummies to scare off thieves and kids screwing around. Only the front and back ones are for real." I find what I'm searching for. "Okay. Here we go. This will go quicker with two sets of eyes. You watch the right monitor, covering the front, and I'll take the left, for the back entrance."

"What are we looking for?"

"My dad. I want to see when he left and when he came back."

"Why?"

"I don't want to say yet. I hope I'm wrong about this. Let's just see."

I start rewinding the coverage. The black-and-white video shows the lobby and front door on the right, and the back exit, with a view of the parking lot, on the left. I speed the video up till I spot Dad returning to the Zoo. The time code says that was twenty minutes ago. I write it down on a Post-it note.

"Okay. Now I want to see when he left this morning. Let's try going back an hour."

I key in the time I want to check, and the screen jumps to show the views from earlier.

"The truck's gone. I'll go back another hour." I bring that video up. "Still gone. Now, three hours? Nothing still. And . . . four? There it is."

The pickup is back in our parking space, before Dad took off.

"Let's see what happens when he left."

"Why?"

"Just watch."

Stick sits on the edge of the desk, focused on the screen, while I key the footage from behind the desk. I hope that I'm just being paranoid, but if I spot what I think I might, I want Stick here to tell me he's seeing what I'm seeing. That I'm not crazy.

I fast-forward the video. We watch people rushing in and out. The Zoo is like a United Nations, with tenants of all colors and nationalities. Vega shows up in the wreck of a car she Frankensteined together from parts discarded by the garage where she works. Shopping-cart Dumpster divers go by.

Minutes zip by on the timer. I barely blink, waiting. Then—

"There!" I slow everything down as Dad comes out the back door.

Walking with that little hitch from his old injury, he strides toward the truck.

"What's he got there?" Stick asks.

Oh no! I wanted to be wrong. But Dad's carrying a big duffel bag. Whatever's in it must be heavy, because he's leaning to his right.

He opens the truck door and heaves the bag in front, takes a few moments to look around the lot and the alleyway. Like he's wondering if anybody has seen him. Then he leans on the open door with his head bowed as if catching his breath. Finally he gets in. But nothing happens, he just sits there as the time code shows a minute go by, then two, then three.

I walk around the desk to stand close to the monitor, focusing on the shadowy form behind the wheel. After five minutes, with me and Stick watching silently, the truck starts up and pulls out, disappearing down the alley.

The breath I've been holding comes out in a shudder.

"You saw that?" I ask, my voice choked.

"Yeah. So what are you thinking? What's in that bag?"

"The body."

Stick's eyes go wide.

I step back to the computer and rewind till I can freeze-frame on Dad carrying the bag. It's big enough, and heavy enough. And the way he's acting in the video . . . His face a shadowy blur, he seems unrecognizable.

Who are you? What have you done?

"And the mud on his boots?" Stick asks.

"I think he buried her."

13

WE'RE ON THE road. Stick's driving. He got Vega to lend us her car for the afternoon.

"You dent it, I'll dent you," she warned him. Like you'd even notice one more ding on this wreck.

I have the window down, to feel the wind on my face and keep me awake. Long time since I slept, and everything's got a dreamlike haze to it.

Stick pulls onto Highway 400, heading north, out of the city. We're following a trail. After seeing the video of Dad loading that bag into his truck, driving off and returning later without the bag—knowing in my gut what must have been inside—I sneaked upstairs for the spare keys to check inside the pickup. We found no sign of the duffel bag, just more muck on the floor mat.

But we found something better when I searched through today's history on the truck's GPS.

We know where he went.

As we drive, I fill Stick in on what I discovered in the logbooks earlier, and we run through some ideas.

"So if your grandfather did the work, sealing up the chute with the girl inside—if he's the killer, then why is your dad doing this? Why cover up for his old man?"

"Who knows why? But . . . I've been replaying how the weirdness with Dad all started, when I first told him about the body in the basement, how confused and surprised he was. I don't think he was faking that. The lies later were more obvious now that I look back. But his initial reaction was shock. I really don't believe he knew the girl was there, buried in the wall all these years."

"But why hide his father's crime when the guy's been dead so long?"

"There's got to be more to it. Maybe my dad was involved somehow. Maybe he's been keeping it secret since then."

I check my cell phone for the GPS memory I copied from the truck, with the map of where Dad went and the coordinates of his final destination.

"How far are we going?" Stick asks.

"About forty miles north, before we get off the highway. Then he drove some back roads out to nowhere. There's no place marked anywhere near there. Guess that's the point, an out-of-the-way hiding spot. It says he stopped there for over an hour. Long enough to dig a hole deep enough."

"What are we gonna do when we get there?"

"Not sure. I'm just taking this step by step."

"Yeah? What if your next step takes you off a cliff?"

"That's why I've got you, Stick. To pull me back."

He puts his hand on my knee, and I cover it with my hand. It's a tight fit for me in here; even with the seat cranked all the way back, my knees are pressed to the dash. I can only drive in Dad's truck, set up for our size. Don't know how I'll ever ride in it again if there really was a body in that bag, tossed up front. Don't know how I'll do anything.

The day is clear and cool, and with it being Sunday there's no real traffic. We're making good time.

"Up here is where we turn off."

After ten minutes on the paved back road, the map says to make a right. There are no signs out here, and the road was nameless on the GPS, but it's taking us where we're supposed to go. When the road becomes just wheel grooves in the dirt we keep on it, till we're bumping over uneven ground without even a hint of a path.

"You sure this is the way?" Stick says. "How far do we go? I don't want to crack an axle and break down out here. Vega would slaughter me."

"We're real close. Stop up ahead, before those trees."

When Stick kills the engine, it's dead quiet. Nothing for miles. Not a soul.

"Dad parked for about an hour," I say. "One hundred yards straight that way."

I open the door and get out, stretching my bad knee. It's aching from being cramped up in the car. My shoes sink in the damp earth. Stick scans the ground.

"Tire treads," he calls out. "Fresh ones."

The marks are clear, pressed deep. We follow them toward a wooded area and find where Dad parked. End of the line.

The clouds have closed in, graying the landscape.

I spot Dad's footprints leading to a stand of birch trees. I walk next to them, matching their long stride.

The birches are skeletal without their leaves, and white as bone. The bark peels from the trunks in thin sheets, like the pages of a book.

The prints end where years of fallen leaves carpet the ground. Walking among the trees, I search for any sign of disturbance. But I don't notice anything, until my shoes sink deeper into a soft patch.

I stop. The leaf cover is lighter here, and the earth shows through in loose clumps, as if it's been freshly turned.

I reach for a fallen branch and use it to sweep away the scatter of leaves, revealing a four-foot-long area of broken ground.

"This is it," I say.

"What now?" Stick shakes his head in disbelief.

I've come this far, I need to know for sure. "Now we dig."

He stares at me wide-eyed.

After discussing how to do it, we head back to the car to find something to dig with. In the trunk there's a spare tire, some tools and two hubcaps. Stick takes one hubcap and hands me the other. "Better than nothing."

We start shoveling with the caps, hunched over opposite ends of the spot. With the earth so loosely packed, it doesn't take long before there's a good-sized hole and piles of dirt heaped to the sides. Dad did a thorough job. We have to go deeper.

After a few minutes, there's room for only one of us in the hole. It's too small for me, so I step out while Stick scrapes deeper.

"Got something," he grunts as he brushes a final layer of dirt clear.

"Get out. Let me see." Stick climbs from the hole and I crouch down inside it. He's uncovered some kind of cloth. I study it. There's a strangely familiar pattern on it, bright yellow sunflowers against a sky-blue background. It takes a moment before it hits me.

That's my old sunflower blanket, from when I was little. A thick winter one I haven't used in years, stuffed away in a closet and forgotten. Seeing it here is surreal.

"What is that?" Stick asks.

Takes me a second to find my voice. "Blanket. It's mine."

He leans over, peering in. My hand is shaking as I reach out. When I touch it, my brain is flooded with memories of lying beneath this blanket and counting the flowers as I fell asleep. The softness of it under my fingertips is so familiar. I pull the blanket back.

The edge comes free, showing me what's beneath. A tangle of dark matted hair. Then the face.

I let go of the blanket and sit back on my heels.

"Wow," Stick whispers. "Wow."

When I stand up, I have to lean on a pile of dirt to keep from falling. My hand sinks into the cold soil. Feels like I'm going to collapse, can't get enough oxygen. I look away, up through the branches of the birch trees at the darkening sky. Not sure how long I'm gasping for air before I feel Stick's hand on my shoulder.

"You okay?"

"No."

"Want to get out of there?"

I nod and he gives me a hand up. I hang on to him till my legs can hold me.

"You see that? See her?" I need him to witness this nightmare.

"Can't believe it, but I see her. What . . . what do we do now?"

The ground feels like quicksand, ready to suck me down and swallow me. I'm panting. I want to run, get away, never look back.

"I don't know, Stick. Don't know."

Can't take my eyes off that tortured face, the lips stretched back to reveal a chipped front tooth.

My legs tremble, which causes an electric shiver of pain from my bad knee. It distracts me and I break away.

"Gonna be dark soon," I say. "Nothing we can do right now. So let's just . . . put everything back how it was. I'll think later. Can you . . . cover her face?"

Stick lets out a shuddering breath, looking as sick

and scared as I feel. He leans over the edge of the hole and pulls up the blanket to hide her again.

Then we shove the piled earth back in the hole. The sun is going down. It's hidden behind the clouds as we pat the mound flat, and I grab an armful of leaves to spread over it. You'd never know we were here, or what lies beneath.

The sweat freezes on my back as I stand.

"Let's go, Ty. Before it gets too dark to find the road." Stick leads the way out of the trees, carrying the hubcaps.

In the car I hug my arms tight, trying to stop the shakes. The headlights bounce over the rough ground as we slowly make our way out in silence. I breathe a little easier when we reach the road again.

I keep flashing back on that blanket, and all the cold winter nights I slept warm and safe under it. How many times did Dad tuck me in?

Sweet dreams, he'd say.

On the highway, the headlights from cars speeding by flare in my eyes, leaving flickering afterimages.

And when I close my eyes, I see sunflowers.

14

WHEN THINGS GO *bad, get busy.* That's what Mom says.

After I hurt my knee I didn't leave the apartment for days, just limped around, depressed. Mom got me moving again. I was damaged, not done.

If I just surrender now and hide out in my room this whole mess will drown me. So I keep going as if this is any other day.

When I got home last night with Stick, two days of no sleep caught up with me and I crashed. I collapsed in bed and blacked out for eight hours. Dreamless, thankfully.

Now, I pop a painkiller to take the edge off the ache.

And I get busy. Acting normal. I have an appointment with my physical therapist. I'm sticking to my routine, so I do my stretches and sneak out to the kitchen for my morning shake.

Mom's scrambling eggs, and Squirrel's at the table chattering away, reading from a schoolbook about how the first astronauts were monkeys.

"Astrochimps, they called them."

"You want some eggs?" Mom asks me.

"Just this." I toss a couple of bananas in the blender with chocolate milk and protein powder.

"Missed you at dinner yesterday."

"I was out with Stick."

"Enjoying your break?"

"Sure. Joy." I fire up the blender.

No sign of Dad. While I've been hiding from him, he seems to be avoiding me too. Out early on the job, home late. When we do cross paths, he barely makes eye contact and doesn't speak much more than a grunt.

As I gulp down my shake, Squirrel shows me a picture of a monkey in a space suit.

"You want to be an astrochimp when you grow up?" I ask him.

"Astro-mountain-climber," he tells me. "Because it says here they got mountains on Mars bigger than anywhere."

"Where you off to today?" Mom asks as I put my glass in the sink.

"I've got a torture session for my knee."

"Right. Good luck with that. Going to be home for dinner?"

"Maybe not. I'll grab something."

I leave her listening to Squirrel's plans for Martian mountaineering.

While I'm changing in my room I get a text from Roxy, a shooting guard on my team. Our top scorer, sharp and speedy—Rocket Rox. She's putting a pickup game together down the block on the courts in Moss Park.

Get in the game, girl. It's Tiny Time.

I send back: *Can't. My knee's still in rehab. But you go rock and shock.*

It's been tough watching my team play from the bench. We've been on a losing streak since I went down. Missing me—our monster in the middle. *Watch and learn,* Coach says, because I'm still kind of new to the game. But I'm a bad student on the sidelines. Can't stay still. I need to be on the court battling with my girls. And I was getting some serious attention from the scouts before I got hurt. Don't want them thinking I'm damaged and done. Gotta get back in.

I head downstairs.

In the lobby, Celia is sitting on the bench by the mailboxes, gazing out at the street.

"Hey, Celia. You're up early."

"I get up early and stay up late. Don't want to miss anything."

Her smile makes about a thousand wrinkles in her ninety-one-year-old face. Her skin is deep brown and her hair has gone all snowy, as white as the false teeth she's flashing at me. She likes to watch the world go by, from here or at the coffee shop on the corner. She's like our local historian and nosy neighbor, sitting by her fourth-floor window and keeping track of the comings and goings. She's been living here forever. Older than the building, older than pretty much everything.

"Can you feel it?" she asks, her thick glasses making her eyes look big and owlish.

"Feel what?"

"The building. It's settling in for winter. Creaking and cracking all over, like an old lady. Like me. Bracing itself for the deep freeze."

"You talk like it's a living thing."

"It is, supergirl. With a steel skeleton and cement bones. Pipes for veins, wiring for brains. Dusty ventilation shafts for lungs. And windows for eyes."

She makes me smile for the first time in days. Celia's always hanging around telling stories to anyone who cares to listen.

"Where's its heart?" I ask.

"We're its heart. You and me, and everyone within these walls. Without us, it's dead and dusty."

Her words make me shiver. If this place is alive, with all of us a part of it, Celia must be its memory.

I wonder what she knows.

"You remember the old super? My grandfather?"

She frowns, spawning more wrinkles, dark eyes huge behind her lenses. "Mad Dog?"

"Yeah." Guess his wild temper was no secret. "How bad was he?"

She shakes her head. "Nasty and rabid. Crazy as they come."

Crazy enough to kill?

"How do you mean?" I ask.

"He knew how to hide it behind a laugh and a grin. But he was rotten to the core. He was a handsome devil, but a devil first. And . . . well, I don't like to gossip."

I hold back a smile. That's her favorite hobby. Life in the Zoo is a big soap opera, where every floor has its dramas, scandals and heartbreaks. And Celia knows them all.

"But since it is your family, your blood, I guess I can tell. Your grandmother, Maggie, was a friend of mine. She went through hell with that man. Maggie was pretty, in a fragile kind of way, a breakable beauty you might say. And Lord, how he broke her. Not so it would show, he was careful about that, left her face alone. She always wore long sleeves and scarves to cover the bruises." Celia rubs her arms, like she feels a chill. "He controlled her. But she sneaked out now and then and we'd have coffee. She never talked about how he hurt her. Anytime I tried to bring it up, she'd shrug it off. Maggie knew I knew, and I guess that was enough for her, so she didn't feel alone in it."

Celia sighs. "Maybe I should have said something to somebody. But I didn't want to make it worse. He would have been the death of her, if he hadn't dropped dead himself. Sooner or later even the devil gets his due. I miss her. We had some good talks. She kept a little secret garden up on the roof, and we'd sit up there with a thermos of coffee. Been ages since I saw her, but I understand why she never comes back here. Guess it's haunted for her."

So my grandfather was a monster. But was he a murderer? How *mad* was he, and how far did he go?

Celia leans back to look up at me. "You're so much like her—long and tall, the both of you." She reaches over and gives my hand a squeeze with her cool dry fingers. "When you see her, give her my love, super-girl."

She calls me that not just because I'm the super-intendent's daughter, but like she's told me before, *I see big things in you, big girl.*

"See you later, Celia."

"I'll be here. Always have been."

Stepping out into the sun, I wave back to her in the shadowy lobby of our haunted house.

15

ME AND STICK are shooting hoops behind the Zoo, in the back alley court Dad set up a couple of years ago when I started playing. Our court, with lines sprayed on the asphalt, is bordered by a row of Dumpsters and parked cars.

I take a midrange shot that clangs off the rim and Stick chases it down.

"Damn, I'm rusty."

"You've been out a few weeks. Just got to get your touch back." Stick dribbles around some potholes. "What did the therapist say?"

"I've been resting it too much. I need to keep exercising, and focus on my flexibility."

My last MRI showed the partial tear was healing nicely. But if I try to jump or pivot, my knee feels like it's going to buckle and give out. My physical therapist forced me into some wicked stretches and twists.

"It's a good hurt," she told me. "The hurt of healing."

And I laughed, wincing. "Does that line actually work on your other patients?"

"Not really. But you need to hear it."

So I'm working out, feeling the good hurt.

Stick passes me the ball. "You know, Ty, I can help with your flexibility. You need a massage, I'm there. These hands are at your service. I squeeze to please."

"Sorry, Stick. Not in the mood. You'll have to squeeze yourself."

I try from the three-point line, but my shot goes wide.

Truth is, I'm not much of a shooter. I'm a blocker and a banger. The beast you have to move to try and score.

Coach wants me back in the game. We're getting beat down low, outmuscled in the paint. That's Tiny's turf. But worse than that, with me out, we're getting beat up—pushed around and intimidated. Because there's more to my game than guarding the basket. I guard my girls.

When the other team takes a cheap shot at us— throws an elbow, or slams one of our players to the hardwood, nailing us with a flagrant foul, they need to know there's going to be payback. That's my job. Not to go dirty, or to get ejected. But to foul them hard enough that they get it: take my girl out, I'll take you down.

Stick fires one from long range and sinks it. "And the crowd goes wild."

By *crowd* he means our audience of pigeons and crows scavenging from the Dumpsters.

"So, I was thinking, Ty. And I've got some theories."

"Yeah?"

"About the girl. Why your dad went and buried her."

I stand by the free throw line, with Stick under the hoop to feed the ball back to me as I practice my foul shots.

"Let's hear them."

"Maybe your dad was scared he'd get blamed. I mean, he's the super in charge of the place. It's even in the log how he was helping out on the job back when the body got sealed in."

My throw clangs off the rim, and Stick tosses it back to me. "An innocent man doesn't do what he's done," I say.

"Okay, so he's covering for his old man, then. Why? Who knows. He was only a kid himself when it happened, and like you say, his dad was a beast. So maybe Teddy knew what his father had done but kept quiet because he was terrified of him. And now the body shows up, and he feels guilty for keeping the secret all this time. Worried he might get charged as like an accessory or something."

I just shake my head.

"You know your father didn't have anything to do with what happened to the girl. That's *evil* stuff."

"Yeah, I know." I say it, and I really desperately have to believe that. So I bury any doubts, telling myself I can't have been that wrong about Dad.

"Okay," Stick says. "So, forget about why he got rid of the body for now. Let's think about the *way* she was killed, how she got cut open. What's behind that? Let me give you my top crazy ideas for motives."

I fire up another air ball, missing by a mile.

"Let's hear them."

"Maybe it was like organ thieves. You know, when they drug you and steal your kidneys for the black market."

"That's an urban myth."

"It happens. I read about it online."

"You fall for everything you see online. Besides, this wasn't surgical. It was mutilation."

My next shot bangs off the brick wall.

"How about if she was pregnant," Stick says. "And somebody did it to steal the baby. Read about that happening too."

I shudder. "Don't put that picture in my head."

I try to focus on the basket and block the image from my mind.

"How about cannibalism?" Stick tosses the ball.

I'm so stunned I miss the ball and have to run it down. Stick's theory is so crazy, I have to laugh.

"So you're saying I come from a family of cannibals?"

"You tell me why then. Why the overkill?"

I can only shake my head.

"Or she could have been killed because she was a snitch," he says. "I mean, this all happened like twenty-five years ago, back when the old gangs ran the block. She could have been some kind of informant, so they shut her up and sent a message to anybody else who was thinking about talking."

Stick has a point. The neighborhood used to be a lot more dark and dangerous, before the cops cracked down and the gangs moved operations out to the burbs. It was a real shooting gallery back then. We still get smash and grabs with the cars in the lot, and there's junkie debris in the alley, needles and broken pipes, but not like the bad old days.

"Hey, Ty. You think there could be more?"

"More what?"

"Bodies."

I stop dribbling the ball, shivering. "Quit putting this stuff in my head. It's like a whole photo album of atrocities you're downloading to my brain."

I try a skyhook, and bang it off the rim. Stick snags the ricochet and walks the ball over to me.

"How about if it was a satanic cult sacrificial offering?" he tries.

I smile down at him, my shorty squeeze. "Well, this place *is* a portal to hell."

He shrugs. "I'm out of great ideas. Guess we got nothing."

"I've got you." I bend and give him a kiss. "That's something."

"And the crowd goes wild."

A car pulls into the lot, crowding our court. A black Cadillac with tinted windows that takes up two spaces as it parks.

"Somebody's got the wrong address," Stick says.

The driver gets out, a bull of a guy with buzz-cut

black hair, a steroid overdose stuffed into a suit and tie. He opens the back door and we see our mysterious visitor.

It's Slimy. Sam Savard, our slumlord.

He drops by only once or twice a year. Named number one on the city's list of worst landlords, Savard owns other notorious dives in Regent Park and some postapocalyptic apartment complexes by Jane and Finch. He's richer than God, and might be older too. He grew up around here, in old Cabbagetown, back when it was a black hole. Savard crawled out of that sewer to become king of the ghetto.

He earned the name Slimy because he's such a sleaze, and too slippery to catch. Charged over the years with every housing code violation, with loan-sharking his tenants and letting drug dealers set up shop, with twenty kinds of fraud and miscellaneous misdemeanors. He gets away with everything, because of whatever deal he made with the devil.

Stepping out of his car, he doesn't look like much. At five foot nothing, bald and skinny, he could be just another fossil from a nursing home. Till you see his eyes. Quick, bright, blue ice. The kind you can feel on you, like I do now—a visual dissection. I try to hide the shiver as he takes in my height.

"You must be Teddy's girl." His voice is a raspy whisper.

I nod. He reminds me of something slithery that you find under a rock and want to look away from but can't. Revolting and fascinating at the same time. He wears a little gold crucifix necklace that winks in the sunlight. Him wearing one is a bad joke, as if he's just daring God to smack him down. His leathery fake tan gives those eyes a laser shine.

"What are we feeding you?" he says, looking up at me with a thin smile. The guy's got no lips, like a lizard.

He doesn't wait for a reply, just heads for the back door of the building, with his driver trailing.

What are we feeding you? As if I'm just another animal in his zoo.

Savard waits as the driver gets out a key and opens the door for him. Slimy will get in and out without leaving a single fingerprint.

"Stay with the car," he rasps at the driver.

Stick's dribbling the basketball as the goon walks past us.

"That ball better not touch this car," the driver rumbles.

Me and Stick glance at each other. Game's over.

"Let's go eat," Stick says.

"Pizza?"

"Paradise."

"Let me just put the ball upstairs."

As we reach the door, Stick looks back at the glaring driver and gives him a little wave.

"Stay," he says. Like the guy is Slimy's dog.

I hustle Stick inside.

"You got a death wish?"

"He'd never catch me. I'm speedy as a roach."

"We stomp on roaches all the time. They're speedy but dumb, like you, boy." We head for the elevators in the lobby. "If you get in a fight, I'm in it too. So that's a death wish for two."

We hear voices coming from the manager's office. Dad's almost shouting. That stops me. He never yells. Then there are the lower tones of Savard. I step closer. Hard to get what's being said. It's muffled by the door.

"Can't . . . no . . . ," Dad's saying.

Slimy talks, inaudible.

Dad responds. "You're not the one who . . . no more . . . it's on me."

Stick's leaning in close when the knob turns. I yank him around the corner, out of sight.

The door opens and shuts. Footsteps, then someone jabbing the elevator button.

"I don't want any part of it," Dad grumbles, low.

"Don't worry, Teddy. I've got it covered."

There's tense silence until the elevator comes. When the doors close, Stick and I come out of hiding.

"What the hell was that about?" Stick asks.

I watch as the readout above the elevator shows it going down to the subbasement.

"What are they doing down there?" he says.

I shake my head.

"Can we sneak around and check?"

I think about it. "Not without them knowing."

"What do we do?"

"Nothing we can do. Let's just get out of here."

Outside, I stop on the front steps.

"Wait a sec." I hand him the ball, take out my cell phone and flip through my photos.

"What is it?" Stick asks.

I find what I'm looking for. "These are the pictures I took of the pages in the logbook, the ones that show when the chute was sealed up. See the initials beside all the different jobs. *TG* for Dad. *DG,* my grandfather. But look at this."

I point to the top of the page, where all the work done and repairs made are authorized with a signature of approval from the man in charge.

SS. Sam Savard.

16

WHO WAS SHE, the girl in the wall?

Stick's got an idea how we might find out.

We're sitting in the Starbucks on the corner of our block. He brought his old laptop—"craptop" he calls it because it's a twitchy piece of tech.

After Slimy's visit gave us more questions and no answers, we go back to basics. Who was she?

"How does this work?" I ask.

"It's simple. We build a face."

Stick found an app online, a digital sketch artist.

"This is based on the program the FBI developed for facial composites. Instead of giving a description to a sketch artist so they can work up a picture of a suspect, the program lets you construct your own, choosing from a catalog of features."

"Like Mr. Potato Head? Stick on some lips, a nose and ears?"

"Exactly. I wish I'd thought of taking a photo of the girl. I was just too freaked. But between the two of us, we should be able to reconstruct her."

"But what are we going to do with a sketch? Go knocking on doors asking if anybody knows her? Put her up on street posts?"

"If we've got a sketch to work with, I could check it against the missing-person notices the police department has online. They've got a link where you can go through years of missing people, and see their pictures. It goes back decades with old cold cases. You don't get much colder than our girl."

"Stick, you got brains."

"And a killer body, don't forget that."

"How could I forget your bony butt?"

"So what do you say? Want to play crime scene, Potato Head?"

"Let's play."

"Can you see her in your mind?"

"I can't stop seeing her," I tell Stick. "But she would have looked a lot different when she was alive."

"I know, but the basic features are still the same."

The program is a multiple-choice kind of thing, where you pick out the parts. We start with the shape of the face. Stick brings up the options.

After studying them, I go with oval. The screen shows a blank mannequin face.

"Now the nose. Very important."

Who knew there could be so many noses? Not just wide or narrow, big or small, but pug, hawk, flat, pointy, bent, with large or thin nostrils.

I get lost in the nose gallery. "I don't know."

"Close your eyes and try to picture her."

I shut my eyes. I do see her.

"There. That's it." I pick one of the flatter ones with a slight flare to the nostrils.

"Good, that's the one I would have gone with."

We move on to the mouth. A tough choice. I saw it stretched open, lips pulled back. How would it look normally?

"Wide," I say. "Full lips."

Stick scrolls through dozens of types till one fits with my memory. It's amazing how much is coming back to me now, and how clearly.

"Her ears were pierced, with a little gold cross in one. And they stuck out a little."

"We'll try that."

The blank mannequin face is more human with each step.

"What are we going to do about the eyes?" I ask. "There's no way to know."

"I guess we can make them brown. That's a safe, neutral color."

For skin tone we choose a warm Latino brown, a shade darker than Stick.

The hair is easy. Black, shoulder length, parted near the middle, and with a slight wave.

Not too wide at the forehead, and a little weak at the chin.

When we're done building, I study the results. "Wow. It's almost like a real person. Like it could be a photo if you didn't get too close."

"I can tweak it some more to make it seem like an actual picture. Add a light source, give it a little shadowing and a gleam in the eyes."

Stick's a wizard with photo fakery. He's always sending me joke shots of himself Photoshopped into exotic places or historical events. He'll splice himself into the background so he shows up as a time-traveling trespasser, a face in the crowd.

"Too bad we can't show her chipped front tooth."

"I'll see what I can do overnight. A little homicide homework."

Sketching her out on the screen, it's like we're bringing her back to life.

"You think this will work?" I ask.

"Worth a shot. What else have we got?"

I've been sunk so deep in what we've been doing that when I look around now, I'm surprised by the crowd in the café, the hum of music and conversations I tuned out. My coffee's cold.

"I'll check for her on the missing-person sites," Stick says.

I stare out the window at the empty street. The road crew has quit for the day, leaving behind that block-long trench. I get a split-second flash of her grave, a hole in the ground where she's buried un-marked and unknown.

"She's not really missing anymore. We know where she is."

"We found her body. Now we need to find her name."

17

THE BEAT WAKES me up. Feels like I fell asleep only minutes ago.

What is that—the road crew already? It's barely light out.

Boom boom boom boom.

I get out of bed and stagger down the hall to the kitchen for some orange juice. The booming comes with me. When I flick on the light, I wince at its brightness.

Boom boom boom. Sounds like they're bombing the neighborhood.

I pour a glass of juice. Then I hear the front door open.

Who's up this early?

Heavy footfalls coming down the hall. Must be Dad. What's he up to now?

Standing at the counter I don't turn when he comes into the kitchen. Too tired. I drink just to be doing something. His steps get closer, then stop right behind me.

Go away. I can't deal with you.

"Tyne." His voice rumbles in my ear.

I try not to shiver.

"Need your help." He's hoarse, exhausted.

"Can't," I mutter. "Too early."

His hand rests on my shoulder, making me flinch. I almost drop the glass. Breathing in, I smell something strange on him. Kind of metallic. Coppery. His touch freezes me. I keep my eyes on the counter.

"We have to clean it up." He sounds groggy, like he's sleepwalking, sleep-talking.

"Clean what?"

Out of the corner of my eye I catch something falling from his hand past my shoulder. A drop of red that lands in my juice. It spreads in the orange, followed by another drip.

Staring down, I see his boots behind me, surrounded by a puddle of crimson on the white tiles. I spin around. My glass shatters at my feet.

He's soaked in blood, head to toe.

"No!" I shout. "What—what's—? You hurt?"

He shakes his head, throwing off a spray of blood. "It's not mine."

He grabs my wrists. "We have to clean up."

He pulls me after him, my feet sliding across the wet floor as I fight to break free.

"Don't!" I beg. "Don't make me."

The red runs off him like he's been swimming in it. The smell is choking me, thick and gagging. I can taste it on my tongue.

Reaching the front door, he throws it open. But there's no hallway. Just the furnace room in the basement, still flooded, but now in blood. Blood pouring from cracks in the walls, holes in the ceiling.

He yanks me forward till I'm knee-deep.

"No! Please!" I shriek. "Let me go! You can't make me!"

Dad leads me to the pump, which is pounding away—*boom boom boom.*

"Don't let it stop!" he yells over the noise.

Grabbing a bucket, he wades in. He goes deeper and deeper. Then he goes under.

I open my mouth to scream. But the floor gives out, and I plunge into the flood. Gasping, I suck it in. Drowning.

GAGGING, I ROLL over to the side of my bed.

Dry-heaving till I can breathe again, I hang my head over the edge.

I'm shaking like crazy.

I sit up and swipe at my damp forehead—slick with sweat, not blood. Still, I can smell it, taste it.

Fumbling around in the gray darkness, I find a half-full can of Coke on my desk and gulp the flat soda.

My brain's been going in circles all day, after the visit from Slimy.

What were he and Dad arguing about? And what were they doing in the basement? Is Slimy involved in the killing? Is that who Dad's covering up for? But why?

Were they going down to visit the scene of the crime, and the hole in the wall? But why would they do that? The body's gone. There's nothing to see.

Questions chasing questions.

I go to the window and suck in the cool night air. The view from here is like a window on another world, looking at the rich new condos with their balcony gardens in the shiny towers rising up around us. The good life, so close I can see what I'm missing.

Stick tried to give me some alternate explanations for why Slimy showed up today. Like he was just here to see the damage done by the road crews, all those cracks in the foundations and the broken pipes. And when Dad was saying he didn't want any part of it, wouldn't do it, maybe he was talking about the way Slimy always covers up problems, hides the damage so he won't have to pay for repairs. Slimy's notorious for hazardous conditions in his buildings. They're death traps, disasters waiting to happen. Maybe this time he was trying to go too far, and Dad wouldn't go along with his plans in case the whole place came crashing down.

Who knows? Can't be sure of anything.

But whatever Dad's done, as long as I'm keeping his secret, I'm in on it too.

Like we've both got blood on our hands.

18

GROWING UP, I never felt poor till I came here.

Uncle Jake's huge house is north of Toronto, in Richmond Hill—Rich Hill, I always called it. It has a pool and hot tub, a three-car garage, a garden and a backyard that's more like a field. And five bathrooms! When Mom told me that, I asked her why so many. She just said, *Because they can.*

Jake is in construction, building condos and subdivisions around the city.

We come here now and then to visit, because my grandmother lives with Uncle Jake and Aunt Vicki. *We* is me, Mom and Squirrel. Dad's a no-show. The whole family used to make the trip on Christmas, so all the Greers could be together. But the past few years Dad has found any excuse to keep us away—bad weather or a bad day at the Zoo, too busy or sick, whatever. The real reason is that Jake gets drunk and things get ugly. They argue. Now Dad keeps his distance from the drama.

But Squirrel loves it here. It's like Disneyland to him. There's a gaming room with a TV so huge it wouldn't fit in our apartment, the pool, dogs to play with, room to run, trees to climb.

"I'm gonna bounce. Gonna bounce," he keeps saying as we drive up to the house. Jake's got a trampoline too.

Mom pulls onto the long driveway. The place always makes me feel like we're showing up in our scratched pickup to clean the pool, mow the lawn or do some landscaping. As we park and get out, two dogs run toward us.

Squirrel races across the lawn to meet the German shepherds. We watch as they lick and nuzzle him. They bark, he barks back. He thinks he's one of them. The lost runt from their litter.

Aunt Vicki waves to us from the front door.

Squirrel yells, "Aunt V, can I go swimming?"

"Too cold. We closed the pool for winter."

"Can I trampoline with the dogs?"

She smiles. "If you can get them on there. Why don't you go around back? It's all set up."

She knows Squirrel is a human tornado, so she tries to quarantine him when we visit, letting him run wild in the yard but keeping him out of the pristine house. He races off with the pack now, and we follow.

This place has a Disney feel for me too, but not the fun-and-rides kind. No, it's more of a fairy-tale vibe. When I was little I thought Aunt Vicki was some kind of ice queen. With skin so pale you can see the faint blue veins at her temples, her winter-sky eyes and long platinum hair, she's perfect for the part. She looks like ice cubes wouldn't melt in her mouth. But Aunt Vicki's not a mean queen, more of a sad and lonely one in her ice palace. The house is always cold, and it feels like a museum, with a lot of beautiful stuff on display but no soul living there. Vicki used to be an interior designer—that's how she met my builder uncle—but that was years ago. Uncle Jake doesn't like her working anymore. She's so thin and delicate, and kind of spacey on her anxiety meds.

I would have skipped this trip, but I wanted to visit Gran and ask her about Mad Dog.

I spot her across the wide backyard in her flower garden, and go over. As I come up on Gran from behind, I find her kneeling in the dirt, like she's digging, or burying something. But when I get closer I see she's just examining some small purple flowers poking up from the earth.

My shadow falls over her and she flinches. She glances up, startled.

"Oh, Tyne, honey. Scared me."

"Sorry, didn't mean to sneak up."

"I just get lost in the little things. Like these crocuses. Last blooms of the year." The flowers show a sunburst splash of orange inside their violet petals, at their heart. "The rest of the garden's gone into hiding for winter. But these brave souls aren't scared of the frost."

She stands up, slow and stiff. Gran's over six feet tall, just a few inches shorter than me. Seeing her is like looking in a time-machine mirror; we share the same sharp features, long nose, high cheekbones. Her green eyes are paler than mine, like a plant that's been growing in the shade. And if you look closely, her left eye is damaged, the pupil wide and permanently dilated. Mad Dog did that to her. She's got an old-lady slouch, from all the years of trying to fit in the world. But still, she looks like me, plus fifty years.

She rubs her hands like they're hurting, and bends to pick up her pruning shears.

"These things make my fingers ache. Too small for me, like everything else. Ever get the feeling this world is made for munchkins?"

"All the time." I smile.

"I used to have some oversized gardening tools that fit my hands. They were my mother's. Never been able to find any like them. Left mine behind when I moved out of the Zoo."

"Well, we probably still have them down in the basement, in storage. You could come by."

She gives a little shake of her head. "No. Can't go back there."

We wander through her hibernating garden.

"Not much to look at now," she says. "But do you want to see something secret?"

"Sure." I'm here for secrets.

Crunching through dead leaves, she leads me over to the gardening shed, which sits tucked away in the shade of an old oak tree. I'm expecting tools and supplies inside. But when Gran opens it up, it's like a door to summer.

Inside it's ten degrees warmer, and brighter than the clear winter day.

"My getaway garden," Gran says. "My escape from the world, from weather and winter."

Sunlamp bulbs are strung up from the ceiling, shining rich yellow light on the green oasis. Rows of potted plants line the walls. With everything blooming, hidden away in this alternate floral universe, it smells glorious.

"Wow!" I say.

"Jake built it for me. Always been good with his hands."

Uncle Jake is a natural at construction. The other half of his job is demolition: he tears old places down to make way for the new. *A maker and a breaker,* he likes to say. Jake's good with his hands, but he's bad with them too.

One of the big fights between the brothers was over what Jake did with those hands.

It's not stuff I was supposed to know, but I overheard it years back by being in the basement of the house at the right time.

Dad, Jake and Gran were talking about what was wrong with Vicki. She kept getting hurt, and not by accident. This time it was a broken wrist.

"I didn't mean it," Jake was saying. "She's just a fragile thing, like she's made of eggshells."

"That's garbage," Dad said. "Maybe you believe your lies, but we don't. Before, you claimed she was clumsy, or she bruised easy. You think Mom can't see the signs, after what she went through?"

"You saying I'm like *him,* the old Mad Dog? Telling me how to treat my wife?"

Things got heated, louder and angrier, till Gran's soft voice broke in.

"Stop it, Jake. Please. For me, stop."

They went quiet then. "Sorry, Mom. It's only . . . I was drinking. Things got out of control."

"It can't happen again, Son. I mean it. I'll be here for you, and for her. But I'll be watching."

And I guess she has been, ever since. Because Vicki doesn't get injured anymore. But you don't have to hit to hurt someone.

Another dirty family secret, but not the one I want from Gran today.

"This is beautiful," I say, basking in the heat of the sunlamps.

"And you can get a tan from the ultraviolet light."

Gran gives me the tour, showing off a rainbow of tulips, irises and sunflowers, before we come to the rosebushes in the back. She stops by one dark bush that looks more dead than alive.

"This one I've had for years, but I've never been able to get it to bloom." The bush is wrapped in a dense tangle of vines and thorns, like it's bound up in barbed wire.

"Looks vicious."

"It's called a *creeper* rose. Notoriously difficult to grow. They're one of the darkest roses, a purple so deep it's near black. Some people find them ugly, because the petals are kind of ragged, with frayed edges. They never bloom for me. The buds just die on the vine, unopened. But I split one open once, just to see. It had a black heart."

She rolls a bud between her fingers, giving me a dark grin.

"Didn't you have a roof garden back at the Zoo?"

"For a while," she says, and sighs. "I'd sneak up there whenever I could. Long as it lasted."

"Why? What happened?"

"Oh. Douglas ended up throwing the pots and planters off the roof. Nearly threw me off too." Her grin turns into a pained smile. "It rained roses that night."

There's so much I want to ask her but can't. She's been through enough hell. How do I ask her if her husband was capable of murder?

"I still keep him around," Gran says, snipping off a wilted bud. "His ashes, I mean."

A cold draft blows through the open door, breathing on the back of my neck.

"Why would you hang on to those?"

"To be sure."

"Sure of what?"

"That he's nothing but dust. That he's not coming back." She runs her thumb lightly over a thorn on a creeper vine. "There must be something wrong with me, that I'm drawn to such nasty things."

I'm surprised she's telling me this. She never talks about *him*. But maybe she feels safe here in her secret garden and is letting her guard down.

I remember what Uncle Jake said to Dad, the drunken remark about how Dad beat his old man in the end without ever throwing a punch, never even fighting back. How Dad had the last laugh. What did that mean? Since Gran's opening up a little, I ask.

"How did he die?"

That freezes her for a long moment, as if she's holding her breath. I feel like I'm on the edge of something. Just when it seems like she's going to speak, the quiet is broken by the roar of a car.

We turn to look out the shed door, back to the house, and I spot Uncle Jake's supercharged red Mustang pulling up the driveway. The engine gets the dogs barking. I glance back at Gran.

"Sorry, honey," she says. "We don't talk about that. Better left forgotten."

What a family. We don't talk about a lot of things.

She takes my arm and closes up the shed. Gran's guard is back up, and as we wander over to the house she chats about my basketball season.

By the time we get there, Jake's showing Squirrel a dog trick, where you make the dogs sit still while you balance a biscuit on top of their nose. And they're not allowed to eat it till you give the command.

"Stay!" Jake says, kneeling as he positions the treats on the dogs' muzzles. Eyes locked on the food, the shepherds go cross-eyed. "See, Squirrel, you've got to show them you're top dog. You're the alpha. Leader of the pack."

Jake keeps them locked in place, vibrating in anticipation for a cruel half minute before he says, "Go!"

And the dogs snap the treats out of the air.

"Do it again! Again!"

"Later, kid," Jake tells him. "Don't want to fatten them up. What kind of name is Squirrel, anyway? Dogs eat squirrels. Everything eats squirrels. I even ate one on a hunting trip."

He grabs my brother's arm and goes to take a bite, making him squeal.

Jake's nothing like my dad. Short and handsome, with black wavy hair and a smile with too many teeth. Green eyes, not emerald like mine, or faded like Gran's; his are the color of money. Where Dad is the silent type, his big brother is the life of the party.

He catches sight of me now.

"Hey, Tiny. How's my girl?"

"Hungry. But not for squirrels, or biscuits."

"Then let's fire up the Inferno." He gestures to his huge barbecue. "Big enough to grill a bull, from hooves to horns. Then we can shoot some hoops. You owe me a rematch."

He's got a basket set up over the garage.

"Don't know if my knee's up to it."

"No pain, no gain."

I don't want to play Jake because he takes it way too seriously. He's always got to win. No playing for fun. *Fun's for fools,* he told me. Last time we played twenty-one, and he was banging and fouling me like it was streetball down in the hood. So I did what I'm built to do—blocked, rebounded and dominated. And beat him. He tried to hide it, but I could tell he was pissed. Still smiling, only more like the dogs when they flash their teeth. He wanted to go again, but I said it was getting late. Jake said, *Next time, Tiny.*

Heading for the house now, he calls back to me, "I'm getting some extra Raptors tickets for their game against the Knicks. If you drop by my office you can pick them up."

"Sounds great."

I could never afford to see a game, but Jake scores free tickets through his business, so I can take Stick and see how the pros play.

When Jake comes back out he's carrying a platter heaped with thick steaks.

He ignites the Inferno. "So fresh they were breathing yesterday."

"Meat doesn't breathe." Squirrel watches as his uncle brushes sauce on the steaks.

"Well, you're breathing, squirrel meat." Jake reaches out with the brush and dabs the back of Squirrel's hand. "Don't get too close to the fire or you'll be lunch."

Squirrel giggles like crazy, licking the sauce off.

Jake works the grill while Vicki and Gran watch Squirrel show off one of his tricks, walking on his hands with Mom holding his legs steady.

Later, we sit down to lunch on the patio, chatting and laughing.

Like a normal family, with nothing to hide.

19

"SHE'S NOWHERE," STICK says as we grab a seat on one of the stone benches in front of city hall.

They're getting ready for the big New Year's Eve bash in the Square tonight, with a stage set up for the countdown concert.

Stick had an uncontrollable craving, so we took the subway over here, to the food trucks that line the street. Today's craving was for a big pile of poutine, a French-Canadian delicacy: a mountain of fries covered in cheese curds and drowned in hot gravy so everything melts together into a gooey, disgustingly delicious mess.

"I checked back through years of missing-persons reports," Stick says. "No sign of her. Nothing close to our sketch. And I looked at the RCMP's missing site. Lots of lost girls, but none fitting our description."

Stick stuffs his face and his eyes roll back in ecstasy. I'm having a jumbo chili dog from Spicy Stan's, which advertizes a hundred hot sauces with a heat meter chart on the side of the truck. The temperature rating I go for is "fire-breather." That's high, but nowhere near "suicidal scorcher." Still, my dog is making me sweat and tearing my eyes up.

"I guess that means she was never reported," I say. "Maybe an illegal alien? Or could be a prostitute. They disappear and nobody goes looking for them."

They're disposable. Like a body stuffed in a trash chute.

I look out over the wide reflecting pool that the city has turned into an open-air skating rink for the winter. I took my first ice steps here when I was little and Dad showed me how to skate. With me slipping and squealing as he held my mittened hands, I shuffled and slid, struggling to stay vertical. Whenever I started to fall, Dad would lift me up and keep me from crashing to the ice.

"But I had some luck with the brand," Stick says.

"You find out what it means?"

"Yeah. That design, with the skull and the flower, it's called a memento mori."

"What's that?"

"It's Latin for 'a reminder of death.' Like, don't forget you're going to die one day—that kind of thing. There's all kinds of these memento designs that show up in old paintings and manuscripts and stuff. Some people get it tattooed as a kind of personal motto, like you better live it up today 'cause you're dying tomorrow."

"So it's not a gang thing, or some death cult?" I ask.

"No. But it can mean different things to whoever gets it. From a positive 'seize the day' message to something gloomier, like 'I'm a dead man walking.' "

"Or dead girl. And how about those letters, *MIVEM*? I searched everywhere and came up blank."

"Me too. Must be really obscure. I posted it, with the flowering skull, on some online bulletin boards, asking for help."

"What, you're crowd-sourcing our investigation? Tell me you didn't post the photo you took of the finger."

"I'm not that dumb. I sent out a tracing of the design, and the lettering. I figure somebody somewhere will know what it means. Just waiting to hear."

There's something about that design that feels strangely familiar, like I've seen it before. But when I reach for that faint memory, it vanishes. Maybe it was long ago, or I barely noticed it at the time.

Stick stirs his cheesy fries. "How about you, Ty? Come up with anything?"

"I've been digging through old newspaper archives from the *Toronto Sun* and the *Star* for stories about the neighborhood, back around the time that the body got dumped. It used to be a real shooting gallery. Highest crime rate in the city."

"That's why they call it the 'Big Red Dot.' "

Our neighborhood got that name when the city made a map showing where crime was concentrated, with little dots indicating the worst areas. There was a huge cluster right on top of us—we were the big red dot.

I nod. "Before they cleaned up the block and cracked down on the crackheads, and the gangs moved out to the burbs."

"So, you find any more murders? Dead girls?"

I gulp some lemonade to cool my tongue, but I'm still breathing fire. "No. There was a lot about Slimy, though. Savard had a hand in every dirty deal, but nobody could prove it."

I get queasy just thinking about him. He has been Dad's boss forever, though I can't see my father ever covering up for him. But I can see Mad Dog working with Slimy, who let the gangs and dealers set up shop on the block, and taking his cut. My grandfather was probably paid off to look the other way.

Years after the gangs were exiled and Dad became super, we used to get break-ins down in the basement of the Zoo. There were still people who thought that when the dealers cleared out, they left some of their stash behind, so they'd sneak in at night to search.

I reach over and steal one of Stick's fries. We take in the winter sun, enjoying the mild weather with the crowds.

"Doesn't seem real," he says. "If I hadn't seen her with my own eyes I'd never believe it. There's no way your dad had anything to do with that. I mean, you saw how he buried her, wrapped in that blanket like he was trying to take care of her. There's got to be some way to explain it."

"If I can't find it, I'll lose everything we ever had. Every good moment and memory. It'll make it all a lie." I shake my head. "I can't have been that wrong about him my whole life."

"So where do we look now?" Stick asks. "I'm at a dead end."

I think about the sketch we made, bringing the girl back to life.

She must have had a family, must have had someone who cared somewhere, right? Or maybe not. But even if nobody reported her lost, even if she wasn't missed, somebody's got to remember her.

And maybe I know who.

20

CELIA'S HAD HER eyes on the street for ninety-one years.

I know her favorite spots, where she likes to spy on the world going by. When she's not watching from her window at the Zoo, Celia likes to sit at the Starbucks on the corner in the morning, nibbling at a muffin one crumb at a time like the old bird she is. Then she creaks on her cane down to the library two blocks away, where she reads newspapers and chats with everybody. On a sunny afternoon like today, during this weirdly warm *winterruption,* I'll find her nearby, in Moss Park.

And that's where I spot her, perched on a bench under a huge old oak, watching the local wildlife— a couple of teenagers lying on the grass, guy on top of girl, lips locked.

Celia sees me coming.

"Hey there, supergirl."

"Hey, Celia. Soaking up the sun?"

"While it lasts. Warming these bones." She smiles,

flashing her brilliant false teeth. "You're looking tired, girl. Not sleeping?"

Celia doesn't miss a thing. "Rough nights. Rough days."

"Sit with me. I can't talk with you so tall. Give me a crick in my neck."

I join her on the bench.

"Taking in the view?" I look over at the lovers.

"Mating season is every season when you're young. It's a force of nature. But those two won't last."

"How can you tell?"

"She was with another guy just last week. They were arguing, she was crying. Then they made up, and broke up again, in the span of an hour. This boy is new, but she'll relapse to the old one. They had real chemistry. This boy's trying too hard."

I notice Celia's feet swinging as she chats; they don't even touch the ground, she's so short.

"You can tell all that from here?" I ask.

"Seen it a thousand, thousand times. Different faces, same story. So many seasons, loves come and gone. I know, because I've had my share. Don't look so stunned. I wasn't always old. Been married twice, and buried both husbands—not that I had a hand in their passing. The first was my true crazy-deep love, the second was bad to the bone."

Celia peers at me with her dark antique eyes, magnified by her thick glasses. I can see stories in them, waiting to be told, and I wouldn't mind hearing. But I'm here for another reason.

We look up at the sudden riot of shouts and screams

from the playground across the park. This is where the herd of Zoo kids comes to run wild. Even from this distance I spot the flash of coppery-red hair that must be Squirrel. You can pick him out of a crowd by it, like a new penny in the sun. He owns the jungle gym here, daring his buddies from the block to match his acrobatics while Mom watches.

I turn our talk in that direction.

"Have any kids, Celia?"

"Never been blessed."

None of her own, but she's like a great-grandmother to all the building's kids.

"Maybe you can help me with something?"

"What's that, honey?"

"Well, I was looking through a box of old family stuff and I found a picture of a girl with my grandfather. I was wondering if you might recognize her from around the neighborhood, back about twenty-five years ago. Can I show you the photo?"

"Sure thing."

On my phone I pull up the virtual sketch Stick and I built.

"Here she is. I cropped my grandfather out of the picture."

I hand my cell over, and Celia squints at the screen through her thick lenses.

It's a masterpiece. Stick added light and a gleam to the girl's eyes, creating the illusion of reality. And he worked his magic to give her a smile that shows off that chipped front tooth.

Celia studies the image, and I hold my breath,

hoping. She starts to shake her head but then brings the screen in close.

"Maybe. I have a dusty memory of a girl like this hanging around the building. It's been so many years. But I seem to recall a girl who used to cover her mouth when she smiled to hide a broken tooth. She didn't live in the Zoo. I'm sure of that." Celia looks a little longer. "I think she might have lived down our block, in the Weeds."

That place was demolished over a decade ago. They called it the Weeds because it was like a drug-dealer department store. *Different floors for different scores,* they used to say. It was famous for its weed. When they tore the place down, the workers had to wear full hazmat gear, with gas masks, because of the chemical contamination created by the drug labs.

"So, what are you thinking?" Celia asks. "That your grandfather had a girl on the side? A young thing like this?"

"Don't know. Never knew him. But you did. What do *you* think?"

"He always had eyes for the girls, and he was a real looker, in a devilish way. There was talk he was running around on your gran, but I never heard with who. And I don't like spreading rumors." I hide my smile. "Truth is, I always found your grandfather cold and creepy, but I can see some foolish girl falling for his charms. Your gran fell for him, and she was no dummy. Some saw him as a catch." She hands me back the phone. "What are you doing? You looking for this girl?"

With those big eyes of hers she sees there's more than what I'm saying.

"Guess I just have questions," I say.

She nods, understanding, being a curious soul herself.

"But, supergirl, take it from someone who's seen everything twice over and seen too much—sometimes it's better to be left with questions. Because you might not like the answers."

21

TALK TO ME. *Show me the way.*

I stare at the finger in the bottle, begging it to point me in the right direction.

It's getting late and I'm sitting in my room, in front of my computer, at a digital dead end.

MIVEM. The brand scorched into the girl's skin. What does it mean? A word? Name? Secret code? I've put it through every online language translator, dictionaries and encyclopedias, even phone directories, to see if it's some kind of last name.

But it's nowhere.

I tried it as an anagram to see if it might be a letter-jumble code, but it spells nothing no matter how I look at it.

MIVEM. For days it's been running through my brain, a riddle without an answer. Stuck in my head when I fall asleep and waiting for me when I wake up. Driving me crazy.

I'm about ready to give up. I try it in the search

engine one more time, thinking of how to refine my search. But I type it wrong.

And find something. *IVEM* gets some hits.

No way. What's this?

It's an acronym, for a phrase in Latin. *In vita et mors,* which means "in life and death." I click deeper and—

Yes! There it is. *MIVEM,* an older variation of the phrase.

Meum in vita et mors. MINE IN LIFE AND DEATH.

It's supposed to be some kind of vow, or a pledge. Centuries ago people used to get it inscribed inside wedding rings. A message of love and possession, meaning "You belong to me."

I hold the finger up to the screen. Together with that flowering skull—the memento mori, reminder of death—it makes for some kind of dark promise.

I feel a rush at my discovery, and a chill.

So—*who did you belong to in death?*

My phone buzzes, startling me.

I lost track of time, and I remember I've got my own promise to keep. A midnight rendezvous with Stick.

—

IT'S NEW YEAR'S Eve, and I meet Stick on the roof for our own private party. There's a huge fireworks display over Lake Ontario to ring in the new year, and from the roof of the Zoo we can see the top part of it lighting up the sky. It's not much of a view, but it's all ours.

Like last year, we've got our little love-nest camping tent set up for after, so we can celebrate. It might sound wrong with everything that's gone down these past few days, but I need the escape, to be with Stick and feel something that doesn't hurt.

Right now, we huddle up close on lawn chairs, surrounded by a galaxy of city lights. Stick brought pizza, and I came with chips and the boxes of chocolates some tenants give Dad at Christmas. As we feast, I fill Stick in on cracking the code, showing him on my phone what I found.

"Mine in life and death," he says. "That's one vicious valentine."

"Burned into her. Saying *I own you*. Like livestock."

The night is clear. It's cold but not freezing. Still, I've got the collar of my coat up against the wind. And Stick brought a thermos of hot chocolate.

"So, if Celia's right and she was a Weeds girl"—he scrolls down the page on my cell—"what's she doing with Latin on her? Seems kind of strange and obscure. Who branded her?"

I've been wondering at the weirdness of it too, and something comes to me now. "You know, I remember my grandfather went to St. Mary's, a couple of blocks over. It's a Catholic school. They probably teach the kids some Latin."

"How about your dad? He go there too?"

"No. Dad went to the same public schools as you and me. But when I was looking into Slimy, I saw that he's involved in church charities. Maybe he's trying to buy his way into heaven. He goes way back to the old Cabbagetown slum, when I think most of the schools were Catholic. He always wears that little gold cross around his neck. I'm surprised it doesn't burst into flames when it touches him."

"So both Slimy and Mad Dog might've known a little Latin. *Mine in life and death.* Sounds like a threat, not love."

Reaching in my pocket, I pull out the pill bottle. In the glow from my cell you can just make out the flowering skull on the finger.

"You carry that around with you? That is the creepiest thing ever. You think we can make a wish on it?" Stick says, with a shaky laugh.

"It's not like a lucky rabbit's foot. The only luck this is going to bring us is bad."

But I guess I have been wishing on it. Asking it to show us the way, and letting it lead us deeper into the dark.

A loud boom makes us both jump. The sky flashes with a starburst of light in the distance. Show's starting up. I put my arm around Stick and we lean in close. Fireworks explode above the towers of the city with a rolling thunder, dazzling and deafening.

Downtown echoes with thousands of voices counting down to—

"Happy New Year!"

As the crowd cheers, with the sky on fire, we start kissing. And can't stop. I lead Stick over to our nest.

Hidden away in the tent and cocooned together in a sleeping bag, we don't stay cold for long. Our height difference doesn't matter here—we find a way to fit.

The world falls away. I lose myself in a fever of forgetting.

And we make our own fireworks.

22

IT'S A NEW year, but the same old chaos over at Stick's place. On one side of the living room his foster mom, Miss Diaz, is watching TV with the volume cranked up to battle with the hip-hop blasting at the other end, where Vega is fixing up a scooter salvaged from the garage where she works.

"This isn't a parking lot, Vega," Miss D says. "Can't you do that outside?"

"If I leave it out back it'll get ripped off. Trust me, I used to be in that business."

"Don't get grease on the floor." Miss D nibbles from a box of Goldfish crackers.

"That's why I laid the tarp out. Don't worry, it's just for a few days while I make this new again. I already got a buyer lined up."

Me and Stick are in the kitchen, where he's digging deep in the freezer to find some lunch.

"Hey, Ma," he says. "All these Pizza Pops are expired."

"Don't mind that. 'Best before' dates are for rich people. Just a scam. Can't go bad if it's frozen."

"Ghetto trash wisdom," he mutters to me.

"I heard that," Miss D calls.

"Sorry, Ma."

"And we're not trash. We're trashy."

Stick rolls his eyes, tossing half a dozen Pizza Pops into the microwave. I look at the photo gallery covering the cupboards. This is Miss Diaz's legacy, her life's work. Dozens of kids she fostered over the years, from toddlers to teens, every color and race. "My United Nations," she calls her family. Stick and Vega are all that's left, with Miss Diaz getting too old to chase kids around anymore.

Stick loads up a plate of the steaming pops and we head for his room, stepping around the tarp where Vega has laid out scooter parts.

She's right about not leaving it out back. If something's not locked down tight, it's gone. The big red dot that covers our block on the crime map reminds me of something I saw on a field trip to the planetarium downtown. The solar system was projected on the big dome, and they showed Jupiter with its Great Red Spot, which is actually a giant never-ending hurricane the size of Earth. With the smash-and-grabs in the parking lot and the midnight traffic of junkies in the alleys, we're a one-block storm that never ends.

"Girl, you're a skyscraper," Miss Diaz says as I pass by. "Every time you come over you've stretched up some more. You ever gonna stop?"

"Hope so."

I remember asking my doctor the same thing when I was twelve. *When do I stop growing? Enough already.*

Stick's got a room to himself now. He used to share it with whatever crowd of kids was passing through. The more kids Miss Diaz took in, the more money she got. They call it foster farming. She played the system, but she was a solid mom.

Stick clears some space on his cluttered desk for our feast. There's a stack of college scholarship forms Miss Diaz is bugging him to finish filling out. He's applying for every kind of assistance since he's eligible for different programs. Stick's a multiracial dream candidate: black, Latino, with a little Irish mixed in (that's where he gets his electric-blue eyes). He's poor, a foster kid, hardship case, ward of the state. He can use all that, dreaming and scheming his way out.

He wants to go into advertising. Stick's a natural at selling himself. He learned early how to read people so he could fit in quick, whatever new place they sent him to. Got a knack for knowing what they want to hear, and getting them to buy him.

But he's taking a break from applications while we get back to work on our investigation.

We're following up on how Celia thought that the girl in our sketch might have lived in the Weeds. If she was local, she must have gone to one of the schools in the area.

So here we are, me with my tablet and Stick on

his laptop, searching for any digital footprint she left behind. All the city high schools have websites, and most have their yearbooks online. You have to pay to access the new ones, but the old ones, going way back, are free.

"Which one you want to take?" Stick asks, stuffing a Pizza Pop in his mouth.

We've got two high schools she could have gone to.

"I'll take Queen's Cross," I say, which is the one Stick and I go to.

We set our searches around the year when she was sealed up in the shaft. We're guessing her age from fifteen to nineteen—hard to tell with a teenage mummy. Who knows what grade she might have been in? We start clicking through pages of high school yearbook photos, thousands of students.

"Wow," Stick says. "This is like time travel to the land of bad haircuts and fashion disasters."

"We all look like fashion victims, seen from the future. I shock myself in the mirror *now*."

We keep searching, and the faces start to blur together. I have to slow down so I don't miss any potential matches.

One familiar face stops me. Dad. In grade ten at Queen's Cross. He's so impossibly young. Grim and serious, as if he's posing for a mug shot. I can read the sadness and worry in his frown, from living with Mad Dog. I wish I could go back and tell him things would get better, that he'd survive.

When I was heading out this morning, I heard

him in the living room, snoring. He was slumped in his chair—the giant's chair, Squirrel calls it, built for our bigness. I stood in the doorway for a minute, watching him sleep. His face was scrunched up, whether in anger or pain it was hard to tell. His whole body was rigid, fists clenched tight on the armrests, like that wasn't a recliner but an electric chair.

The old bear's snore, such a familiar sound to me while growing up. One of my earliest fuzzy memories is of being held close in Dad's arms, falling asleep with him, my ear pressed to his chest, listening to that deep rumble, like the resting purr of some powerful beast. This morning, standing there, I saw his face flinch and his fists tremor, like he was trapped in a nightmare. Looking at his features contorted in such pain or rage, like I've never seen them before, he seemed even more a stranger. What's haunting you? What are you fighting? What have you done?

Then he gasped and stopped snoring. I froze, holding my breath, waiting for him to open his eyes and catch me watching him. What would I see in those eyes? What raw, unhidden emotion? Who is he really? Down deep, what's he capable of? And for a sickening moment I felt scared of him, for the first time ever.

But his snoring started up again, and I could finally breathe. I backed out of the room.

I never want to feel that fear again. It was a second of doubt that left me shaken, questioning whether Dad might have played a part in the killing. I don't want to go there. I keep clicking through the class photos, on and on. I pull another year from the archives.

By the time Stick has emptied his plate and gone through a dozen pudding cups, I catch myself nodding off and glance over at the bed, wanting to crawl in there and sleep.

"Hey," Stick says, startling me.

"What?"

"Think I've got her."

"No way." I slide my chair over to see his screen.

The page shows some casual snaps of kids goofing around at school and making faces for the camera. Stick points to a picture in the corner. Two girls laughing, arms around each other's shoulders. One's a black girl with braids, the other's a long-haired Latina with a wide smile—and a chipped tooth. I grab our sketch and compare the two faces.

A shiver spider-walks up the back of my neck. Our digital drawing is like a ghost twin to the girl.

"That's her," I say. "Who is she?"

The caption on the photo says *Laughing it up in the caf with Rayanne Blake (left) and Lucy Ramirez (right).*

"Lucy," I say.

Turning to the pages of individual head shots, we find her listed as *No Picture Available* with the grade elevens.

"Guess she didn't make it to photo day," Stick says. "Maybe she was dead by then."

We go back to the laughing shot. Strange to see

her happy, living and breathing. With a wide-open dark gaze, warm and shining.

"We got a name," says Stick.

"And maybe more." I tap the girl with Lucy. "If they were friends, she might know something. We know where Lucy ended up. But where is *she* now?"

23

WE CATCH A break and it takes us only twenty minutes to find Lucy's classmate online. Rayanne Blake-Turret has a Facebook page with pictures that match her younger self in the yearbook. She's a librarian with the Toronto Public Library.

After calling around, we find out she works at the main branch downtown.

So we show up with a cover story and a bunch of questions. We call first, and she agrees to talk to us after Stick explains that Lucy is his long-lost aunt—his mother's sister. His family lost track of Lucy years ago and now he's trying to find her.

Rayanne meets us on the ground level of the towering library. The place feels like a hive, with a hollow core, so you can look up and see all ten floors circling the center. There's a low-level hum to the place as hundreds of library worker bees and studying drones speak in quiet voices. Rayanne joins us by the indoor fountain, whose soft gurgling adds to the white-noise hush.

"Wow, Lucy," she says, sitting on the edge of the fountain next to us. "That was so long ago. I haven't thought about her in years. We were friends for a while, back in grade eleven or twelve, before we lost touch. I don't remember her having a sister. Not a real one, anyway."

"What do you mean, a real one?" Stick asks.

"Well, you know, she lived in a foster home with a bunch of other kids. Not her real family. Her mother had given her up."

"Right, of course," he says. "And she was living down in the Weeds?"

Rayanne nods. "Awful place. Good thing they tore it down. Lucy was a sweet girl. Don't know how she survived that place. But I really can't help you. I lost track of her before we even graduated."

"Why is that?" I ask. "She move?"

"Not sure. I never knew what happened. But before she left, I remember she was really excited. She'd met some guy and she was talking about getting out of the Weeds, how he was going to take her away from there. Save her from all that."

"Did you know the guy?"

"No. Never met him. It was all super secret. I think he was older, maybe married or something. Who knows?"

"How much older?" I ask, thinking about Slimy.

"No idea. She wouldn't say, only that she wasn't supposed to tell anybody anything. It was all kind of weird, sudden and strange. And then . . ."

"Then . . . ?" Stick nudges.

"Well, I don't know if this will help you any? And I never knew for sure, but I think he was hurting her."

"How do you mean?"

"She started getting bruised all the time, on her arms and wrists. I noticed some more on her neck, and they looked like choke marks. Sorry, this is probably more than you need to know."

"No, it's okay," Stick says. "I mean, anything you can give me might help us find her."

"All right. Well, she said it was nothing, that she just bruised easily. Then she showed up one day with her finger bandaged. I asked her what happened. She said it was something he did for her, like it was a gift."

That's when she got the brand. Her memento mori, her reminder of death.

"I think it might have been a tattoo," Rayanne says. "But I never saw it. Soon after that she was just *gone*. No goodbye or anything, just never showed up at school again. When I called her place, at first they said they didn't know where she was. Then they told me she'd been sent to another foster home. But I don't know if I believed them."

"And she never told you the guy's name?" I ask.

"No."

"Or anything about him? What he looked like, where he lived?"

She shakes her head. "Only that she was crazy in love with him. And he had a plan for them. I think there was something he wanted her to do for him. Then I guess they were going to run away. Which maybe they did. Who knows?"

"She have any other friends she hung with?"

"No. Lucy was really shy. And she got moved around a lot, placed in different homes. I think she was only at the Weeds for about a year."

Stick glances to see if I've got anything else and I give him a little headshake.

"Well, thanks for all your help," he says.

"Sorry, I don't have a clue where to find Lucy now. But you could try checking with some of the other foster kids she was living with back then. They might have some idea where she ended up. There was a white girl with her at the Weeds, a couple of years older than us. She went to Queen's Cross too. Think her name was . . . Rosie? But they called her Tank. She was a large girl. Not big like you." Rayanne smiles at me. "She was seriously heavy. Cruel name. But school was always cruel." She gets up to go. "Anyway, hope you have some luck finding Lucy. And I hope things worked out for her. She was a sweet thing."

I force a small smile as Rayanne waves and heads back into the beehive. Stick and I stand staring at the fountain.

"So Lucy was a foster kid too," Stick says. "There used to be lots of foster farms on the block. Might explain why she was never reported missing, how easily she vanished. Some places, they don't keep track of when you come and go. And they're used to runaways. It's not like that with Miss Diaz. But some places, they don't care because they get paid by the head, and if they report you gone they lose that money. So they keep quiet and keep cashing the checks."

When Stick talks like this, it hits me what crappy luck life has given him. I remember him showing me his room for the first time when we were little, and the apartment was crammed with kids. All Stick had was a bunk and a drawer to himself.

"Wow. This sucks," I said.

And Stick being Stick, he just gave me his irresistible electric smile, and said, "You kidding? Look what I got. It's like I won the lottery."

And he meant it. Because there were way worse farms than Miss Diaz's. He'd been there. Looks like Lucy had too.

But Stick finally found a place where somebody cared. He got his happy ending. Lucy never got hers.

24

THE HOUSE IS a wreck, with a dirt and gravel lawn, peeling paint and some duct-taped lawn chairs on the porch.

We climb the steps to the front door.

Wasn't hard picking Tank out from the school yearbook. She was a huge girl. Tank's real name is Rosie Williams.

It didn't take long tracking her current whereabouts online.

Rosie's Classy Cats is what she calls her home-based business. She's a breeder of the kind of fancy felines that look like they belong in royal palaces, or in the laps of evil geniuses bent on world domination. *Pure-bred Purr-fection,* it says on her website, showing long-haired fur balls like Himalayans and Persians.

This run-down section of the burbs has a crack-house vibe to it.

Before we get to the door, I notice a chubby little girl sitting on the porch with a kitten in her lap.

"Hi there," I say.

"She's mine. You can't have her." The girl hugs the kitten close. "Mom says I get to keep her 'cause she was born wrong. Got a stub for a tail, so nobody will buy her."

I shrug. "Nothing wrong with that. Who needs a tail anyway? I do okay without one. You don't have one, do you?"

She looks at me like I'm nuts. "No."

"You're great with kids," Stick mutters, and I elbow him in the ribs.

"Is your mom Rosie?"

A suspicious nod.

"She home?"

The girl gets up, keeping an eye on me as she pushes the door open.

"Mom! Customers!"

We wait in the doorway, peering in at a living room crowded with cages and carriers, with a barrier gate just inside to keep the felines corralled.

"Sorry for the mess," says Rosie, coming in from a back room to the howls of a Siamese in one of the cages.

She's not much different from her yearbook photo, still heavy, with small dark eyes and her face flushed red.

"Did you call about the Persians?"

"No," Stick says, taking over to give her our cover story. "I actually came to ask for your help with something."

"Oh yeah? With what?"

"I think you used to know my aunt. Years ago, back in high school when you were living in the Weeds."

Rosie pulls a tuft of fur off her sleeve, a frown creasing her forehead. "Who's your aunt?"

"Lucy Ramirez."

Rosie freezes up at the name before covering by straightening a stack of carriers. She still doesn't meet our eyes.

"Who?" she says.

"Lucy." Stick pulls out a copy of the yearbook picture he printed. "I heard you were both living in the same foster home back then."

Now she looks closely at him, and her suspicion is clear. She glances at the photo he's holding out.

"Who told you that?"

"An old friend of hers from school said you and Lucy were there together, in the Weeds."

"Guess so. There were a lot of kids passing through that place."

"But you remember her?"

"So? What do you want from me?"

I want to jump in and start pressing her for info, but Stick's got his act down, so I let him lead.

"It's just that my family has been trying to find her. They lost touch after she went into foster care when she was in her teens. Do you know what happened to her? Where she went?"

"Can't help you."

"Anything you can tell me that might help us

locate her would be great. The last anyone heard, she was in grade eleven at Queen's Cross."

Rosie crosses her arms.

"What's your name?" she asks him.

"Ricky. Ricky Ramirez. My mother is Lucy's sister."

She glares at him. "Don't remember her having a sister. How did you find me, anyway?"

"An old classmate of hers remembered you, and we saw your site. I just want to know what happened to her."

"No idea."

"Do you remember who else she was hanging out with back then?"

"That's a long time ago, and we weren't close. Don't know anything."

She's nervous now. Sweating. But why?

I can't hold back any longer, so I finally speak up, taking another angle. "We tried asking Social Services, but they don't have any record of Lucy after she was put in the foster home you were in." Of course, I just made that up, trying to shake Rosie into giving us more. "Did she run away, or maybe hook up with someone?"

Rosie focuses on me. "And who are you?"

"Friend of the family."

"Yeah? What's your name?"

I don't have time to make one up. "Tyne. Tyne Greer."

My last name stops her. She stares at me, and I

swear she's spooked. Her face goes a deeper shade of red. She looks cornered.

"Who sent you?"

"Nobody. We're just trying to find his aunt."

"I don't want anything to do with this. Whatever happened was a long time ago. It's got nothing to do with me."

"But I just—" I start.

"No. I'm done. You have to go now."

"But—"

I step back as the door slams in our faces. We're left standing on the porch, stunned.

"Guess we're done talking," Stick says.

"Guess so."

We go down the steps.

"What the hell was that about?" he asks.

"She knows something. Did you see when she heard my name was Greer? She freaked."

Glancing back at the house, I see the little girl peering out the window.

"But why? What's to be scared of? Old Mad Dog is long gone, right?"

I shrug. "*He's* dead and gone. But maybe what happened back then is still living on somehow. I mean, guilt is forever."

25

EVERYWHERE I GO I get stared at. There's no escaping it. Kids are the worst; they can't hide their shock as they gape up at me. Most times I can tune it out. I see the heads turning in my direction out of the corner of my eye and just keep my focus forward, like I don't notice. But it gets old.

I want to be invisible. Not Girlzilla towering above the crowd.

But I catch a break when I'm on the court playing with a team of other tall girls. And when I'm here, in the community center pool. In the water, I'm just another swimmer, only my head above the surface, my body below.

Here I can stretch out to my full length, kicking without hitting anything and swinging my arms wide and long with a smooth stroke as I slice through the water. To me, chlorine smells like freedom.

As I reach one end of the Olympic-sized pool, I kick off the wall and keep doing my laps.

I've been coming to the center three times a week for my knee. It's a perfect workout, one where I don't have to worry about my knee collapsing on me. I'll be back hitting the hard court soon enough, but this keeps my lungs and endurance up.

I can't completely shut my brain down, still thinking a mile a minute, but I can lose myself in the rhythm of the strokes. Outracing the darkness inside me. Reaching for that elusive aquatic Zen, of being here and now and nowhere else.

I swim till my limbs feel like rubber and my lungs burn. It's a strain to pull myself out of the pool, but I'm clearheaded as I hit the showers.

Besides the pool, the center's got workout rooms, an ice rink and two gyms, one with a hard court. As I pass, I peek in at a pickup basketball game and spot two girls from my team. Nobody's calling fouls, so it's kind of a dogfight, with a lot of banging and flying elbows. Everybody's taking wild shots.

"Yo, Tiny!" Roxy shouts to me. Rocket Rox, our best player. She might make the Junior Nationals team, which is way out of my league. "Get in the game. We could use some defense."

I shake my head. "My knee's still recovering."

"Well, speed it up. We're on a nasty losing streak since you went down. Getting murdered on the boards without our big meat."

"I'll be back at practice next week."

"Better be. We miss our monster."

She chases down a rebound as I walk away. Roxy's

right. I need to get back, get noticed by the scouts. Because I only started to play in my junior year, I've been trying to catch up to the other college-bound girls who've been working the scouts and university reps since they were freshmen. I have to push through the pain. I've eased up on the pills, but if I have to up the meds to play, then I'll do it.

I stop in the other gym, where I know I'll find Mom right about now. She comes here twice a week with Squirrel, because one end of the gym has a climbing wall, and he's nuts about it. As a toddler, he started simple, with the table, chairs and counters at home. One day we found him perched on top of the fridge with no sign of how he got there. Then we caught him on the ledge looking out the open window. You're not a flying squirrel, I told him. Growing up as big sister to a death-defying dynamo, I was always on Squirrel watch. Holding him back from traffic and subways, crazies and crack pipes in the alley. His bodyguard, because he could be gone in a blink. Over the edge.

Which is why we have heavy-duty steel-framed solid window screens that give our place a bit of a prison vibe. These days Squirrel sits by the window for hours watching the road crew rip up the street below, playing along with them using his own bulldozers and trucks.

I spot Mom on the bench by the kids' section of the wall, in her workout spandex and sneakers, her coppery hair pulled back in a ponytail.

"Hey, Ty. Good swim?"

I nod. "Good climb?"

"Can't keep up with him."

Squirrel's halfway up the wall, dangling from handholds. He's wearing a helmet and a harness with a safety line rigged up so there's no way he can fall and get hurt. If he loses his grip he'll just hang there swinging till you reel him in.

"He's bugging me to try out the adult wall," Mom says. "Says he wants to go higher and climb with the bigs. But I don't want him getting stuck where I can't reach. The kids' climb is bad enough for me. He's got no fear of falling, but I do."

Squirrel waves to us, hanging by one hand and giggling hysterically.

"Were you ever that crazy?" I ask.

Mom shakes her head. "I took risks when I was young, but not that death-defying."

"So what was it like growing up in the Weeds?"

"Way worse than the Zoo. Dark and nasty."

"Was it always just you and your mom?"

"Yeah. Just us versus the world. Mom worked two jobs, so I was alone a lot. Getting in trouble. I got a job myself as a delivery girl."

She gasps as Squirrel loses his grip and swings by the cord on his harness. Looks scary, but he just dangles in the air for a few seconds before his momentum brings him back to the wall and he digs his foot into a hold, then finds another to grab on to. Without a pause, he continues his vertical crawl.

"I was hoping this thing would help get the Spider-Man out of his system so he wouldn't go climbing everything in sight. But now he's a hard-core height junkie."

Mom's told me a bit about her old "job" making little drug deliveries around the neighborhood. A very dumb thing she did way back when.

"Hard to believe you worked for a drug dealer," I say.

"He was only a small-time nobody in the Weeds—called his place the Fab Pharmacy, because he dealt in prescription drugs. It was an after-school thing some of the girls did. Stuff you do when you're young and desperate and figure you've got nothing to lose. Living in the Weeds, it was impossible to stay clean. Anyway, I was making good money till my mom got suspicious of my new clothes. I told her it was thrift-store stuff, but she was no fool. Mom busted me—actually followed me and caught me with a delivery. She went ballistic. Here she was killing herself working two crap jobs, and for what? So I could be some drug runner? She dragged me with her to go see the Fab Pharmacist and told him to stay the hell away from me."

"Your mom went after a dealer?"

"He wasn't exactly a drug lord. Just a wannabe, a low-level loser. She told him to stay away, and he says, 'Or what, you gonna rat me out to the narcs?' And, well, you never saw my mother's temper, but when you set her off she could get scary mad, in your face. She had a stare that could skin you. So she says, 'No. I won't rat you out. I'll burn your place down with you in it.' I didn't know who I was more scared of right then, him or her. He told her, 'There's plenty more in the Weeds want to work for me.'"

I shake my head, amazed.

"You ever know a girl back then named Lucy Ramirez? Would have been around the same age as you. Dark-haired Latina, had a chipped front tooth."

She frowns, thinking back. "Don't think so. Why? Who was she?"

"Nobody. Just a . . . a relative of somebody at my school who grew up there. Never mind." I switch subjects. "Slimy dropped by the Zoo the other day to see Dad."

"That old snake." Mom shudders. "Sam Savard. Even his name slithers."

"Do you remember him being around the Weeds when you were a kid?"

"Yeah, he'd come by all the time. Liked the girls."

That grabs me. "How do you mean?"

"He'd show up in his black Cadillac, throw block parties for us out back, with barbecues and ice cream, order up pizzas. He had his favorite girls who'd get gift cards and rides around town. The prince of pervs. We all knew what he was after. Some girls went for it, to make some money. Most were sorry they did, after. The cops tried to charge him a few times, but he managed to buy everybody off and keep the girls quiet."

"You never went?"

She gives me a look like I just shocked her, instead

of her shocking me. "God, no. I was wild, but I knew better. Besides, my mother got in his face a couple of times when she saw him hanging around the girls. She never backed down from anybody, no matter how big and bad they were."

"Your mom was fierce? She's always seemed sort of tame to me."

We don't see my mom's mom much. She lives way out on the West Coast.

"You have no idea. She plays the sweet old lady now, but she could stare down the devil. You get on her wrong side, she'll take you out."

I smile at Mom. "Sounds familiar."

"What, like me?"

"Well, you nearly started a riot in the stands during that game where the girl fouled me with an elbow to the throat."

"It was a cheap shot, and that little bitch's mother was sitting in the next row cheering her on."

"That's part of the game. And the girl got ejected. But Dad still had to hold you back from going after her mom."

She shakes her head with a little laugh. "I wasn't going to beat her down or anything, only . . . get in her face. I'm not going to just sit there and watch you get chopped like that. They think because you're so big it's okay. Like you don't feel it. Anyway, do you really think your dad could hold me back if I didn't let him?"

"Guess not. My mom, the warrior waitress."

"Hey, waitress is what I *do*. Warrior is what I *am*."

We look up at my baby bro, creeping along near the top of the kids' wall.

"You coming down?" Mom calls to him. "Ever?"

"Come get me, Mum," he dares her.

She groans. "So what's with the silent treatment you're giving your father? You've been freezing him out."

What can I tell her?

"Just some father-daughter drama. Don't worry about it."

"Whatever it is, fix it. You guys are too close to be apart. Make it right and make up."

"I'll try." That's the best I can do.

Mom puts her helmet on, eyeing the climb.

I get up to go.

"Now," she says, "I've got a Squirrel to catch."

And I've got a killer.

26

GREER CONSTRUCTION.

Strange seeing my last name big and bold, plastered on signs around the site.

Stranger still how two brothers, Dad and Uncle Jake, who grew up in the same place, with the same chances and same everything, turned out so different.

Dad's stuck keeping the Zoo from falling apart while my uncle builds new places and tears old ones down. Construction and demolition—don't know which Jake likes more. He built a dream house for himself and Aunt Vicki, then poisoned it with his temper and drinking.

"Hey, Tiny," Jake calls, when me and Stick show up at the site trailer. "Come on in."

He sent me a text earlier, saying I should drop by to pick up the Raptors tickets he promised the other day. A game is the last thing on my mind, but Stick said we need the distraction to keep us from cracking up.

"Hi, Uncle Jake. You remember Stick?"

He looks up from a desk buried in paperwork, Starbucks cups and boxes of donuts. "Right, your cheerleader. Hey, kid, saw you at one of her games." Jake digs in a drawer. "Here we go. They're good seats—sixth row, center court."

"Thanks a lot."

"Have a donut," Jake tells Stick. "You look like something out of a starving-kid commercial."

Stick never passes on free food, even if it comes with an insult. He grabs an éclair.

"Since you're here, let me give you the tour. See what you're missing."

Jake doesn't mean that in bad way; it's just that he can't help bragging and showing off. And since he's passing out hundred-dollar tickets, I can't say no.

"Grab a hat and I'll take you up to the top. Million-dollar views."

We all put on yellow hard hats—Stick's is perched on top of his springy corkscrew curls—and Jake leads us to the site. The building is still a skeleton, twenty stories tall.

"I keep bugging your dad to come work for me." Up close, I can smell the booze on Jake. Maybe in his coffee? Don't know if I've ever seen him completely sober.

We get on the elevator, just framework with no doors or walls. You can see the street, and Jake's classic red Mustang parked there, falling away as we go up. Whenever Jake drops by the Zoo you can hear him coming. The car's supercharged engine blasts the block like rolling thunder. He comes downtown to see my games sometimes, or to drop off tickets. But mostly he just shows up to show off, parking his muscle car in front of our dump. I've seen Vega checking out the Mustang, and I can tell she'd love to take it for a joyride, straight to the chop shop. Feeling the itch of her old ways.

"I'd make Teddy a foreman," Jake says. "Even get him a deal on a place somewhere nice. Anywhere's better than the Zoo. Everybody's waiting for them to demolish that place—hell, I'd love to do it myself. Nothing like bringing a building down. There's a science to it, knowing where to find the sweet spots, the breaking points. Then what took years to put up comes crashing to the ground in seconds. It's a rush."

He flashes his canine grin.

"They talk about tearing the Zoo down," I tell him. "But Celia says that Slimy doesn't want to give it up."

"Celia? She still breathing?" He sips his spiked Starbucks. "She was always hanging out her window like a gargoyle, spying on everybody."

The elevator clunks to a stop and we step off, into a frigid wind blowing in off the water.

"The penthouse. Yours for five million."

The view is stunning. We're right on Lake Shore Boulevard, where you get the full panoramic view of Lake Ontario, from the marinas and the ferry docks to the port with the big ships. From the CN Tower to the green oasis of Centre Island across the harbor, and the busy little island airport. This place is a pocket paradise of fresh air and freedom in the downtown crush.

"Sweet," Stick says. "When do I move in?"

He smiles at me, forever a dreamer. He can see himself here. Me, I know I don't belong. It's dizzying—not just from the height and staring all the way down through the bare bones of the construction, but also from the jump from one world to another.

"What do you think, Tiny?" asks Jake.

"I think it's amazingly, wonderfully impossible."

"Possible if you fight and bite your way to the top. Like I did. How about you, Stick?"

"I'm in. I can bite."

Jake glances at us standing together and shakes his head. "You two make a crazy-looking couple. What does she do, use you for a toothpick?"

Jake likes to joke, but most times it seems he's the only one laughing.

But Stick's immune to insults. He's had worse and come through smiling.

"She can use me for whatever she wants."

Punching him in the shoulder, I look off in the direction of the Zoo, but it's hidden behind skyscrapers.

"Hey, Uncle Jake, you ever hang around the Weeds when you were a kid? You know anybody from there?"

"Didn't spend a lot of time with the local losers. I set my sights higher, ran with a different crowd."

We watch a small plane buzz by overhead, escaping the city.

"So you wouldn't remember a girl named Lucy who used to live there? Spanish girl, thin, long black hair, had a chipped front tooth?"

He takes a drink. "No. The girls I went for all lived far from the hood."

Stick gives a little shrug. It was worth a shot.

Wherever we look, it seems like Lucy barely left a footprint in the world. Nobody came when she cried out.

Maybe she went unheard back then. But I hear her now.

27

"WHAT IS THIS?" I ask.

Stick's showing me something on his laptop. We're sitting at the desk in his room, and he's devouring a jumbo bag of barbecue potato chips.

"More homicide homework."

On the computer screen is a collection of thumbnail photos of familiar faces, stacked in a pyramid, with the yearbook picture of Lucy at the top.

"Suspects," I read the title.

"Right. I've gathered everybody connected to the case. With the victim on top, then the prime suspects below her, and at the bottom you get the persons of interest."

I lean in to study the three levels of the pyramid.

"This is why you wanted to see my family photo album the other day? To get these photos?"

He nods. "Your family's at the heart of all this. No way around that. And I got the picture of Slimy from a news story online."

Below the sad smiling shot of Lucy, the prime suspects are Slimy, my grandfather Mad Dog Doug and Dad. The image of the old Dog is taken from the only picture in the album in which he appears, at one of Dad's junior high basketball games. My granddad looked a lot like Uncle Jake—that same grin and good looks. Like Celia said: a handsome devil, but a devil first. Next to his picture is Slimy's, all leathery tan and laser-blue eyes. Dad's shot has his playful, scowling "don't take my picture" look from some party.

"Teddy's up there with the primes only because he's involved somehow," Stick says. "But not like he's the one who did it."

My brain won't go *there*. Can't let it. I don't know why Dad got tangled up in this, but I've got to protect him. To save everything we have together. Save him from himself and whatever he's done.

I move on to the persons of interest. "Why the hell is my grandmother there?"

"You say she keeps the family secrets, right? Hides things? She might know what happened. And she's got some potential motives herself."

"Like what?" I ask.

"Like maybe she found out her husband was cheating on her with this girl. She got jealous and confronted Lucy, things got out of hand and she killed her."

"My granny, a homicidal maniac?" I laugh.

"Everybody's got a dark side. And think who your

dad would do it for—get rid of the body. His own mother's got to be right up there."

Gran, with all her secrets . . . But a killer?

"No way." I steal a chip from Stick while I move on to the rest of the lineup. "Who else we got? Uncle Jake?"

"He was living in the Zoo, had access to everywhere. And from what you say, he was trained by the Mad Dog himself. Look what he's done with your aunt. Sounds like a suspect."

"I doubt it. He's a drunk with a temper. But it's a big jump from abuser to psycho murderer. I can't see him going that far. And way back then he would have been only a kid himself—like, sixteen."

"You can be psycho and sixteen. Where do you think serial killers come from? Anyway, he was living under the same roof as your dad and the Dog, so he might have been in on it somehow."

I shake my head. "Who else we got?"

"There's Lucy's foster sister, Rosie." The yearbook shot of Rosie shows the big girl frowning. "She acted real suspicious when we questioned her. First kind of denying she knew Lucy, then admitting it. And that stuff she said: *Who sent you? I don't want anything to do with this. Whatever happened was a long time ago.* She knows something. Maybe she did it, or maybe she helped."

"Yeah, she's a definite maybe. But with all these 'suspects' and 'persons of interest,' we have to ask why my father would cover up for any of them. Why hide their crime? He might do it for family, but for the rest of them? For Slimy? I can't see it."

"Could have been a Greer family crime, all of them playing a part. Each guilty somehow, so there's a conspiracy to keep it quiet."

I look at the last person of interest. No picture, only a black silhouette of a man's head with the name UNSUB below it.

"Who's UNSUB?" I ask.

"That's crimespeak for 'unknown subject.' The one who's not even on our radar. Mr. X. The suspect to be named later."

I put my hand on Stick's shoulder and give him a little shake. "You've watched way too many crappy murder shows."

"Television's my religion."

"Well, start praying to your TV, then. Because we could use some help."

"My bet's on Slimy." Stick taps that snake's face, leaving a red smear of barbecue on him. "We know he was picking up all kinds of neighborhood girls, so he had the opportunity. Like your mom was saying, whenever the cops tried laying charges on him for underage stuff, he'd buy the girl's silence. What if Lucy wouldn't be bought and he had to shut her up permanently? He had access to the Zoo to dump the body."

That wouldn't shock me. But I'm leaning in another direction.

"I say it's Mad Dog. All the secrets. Gran wouldn't tell me how he died. . . ."

Stick tips his head back and empties the last crumbs from the bag into his mouth. "Or the Man in Black. Our UNSUB. It always turns out to be the one you don't see coming."

There's one final option. And it's the worst. What if Dad really did do it? No conspiracy, no covering up for anybody but himself. But I can't go there. That's the nuclear option, the one that destroys everything.

Why he got rid of the body, and however he's tangled up in this mess, I've got to find out. Because what if there's more at stake than my belief in Dad? I need to know what kind of hold whoever killed Lucy still has on him. And if there's some threat out there, I need to protect us—me, Mom, Squirrel and Dad.

"So what's next, Ty?"

We're running out of places to look.

But I'm not done yet. There's one more place I can dig.

28

I TAKE A bus out to Uncle Jake's house, with a gift for Gran.

I need to know what she knows. What happened back then, how the Mad Dog died, and whether he was capable of killing.

I feel guilty, ambushing her like this. But there's no other way.

I went through our basement storage room earlier and found what I was looking for, plus something more that might be the key to Gran.

When I arrive at the house, nobody answers the bell. But Aunt Vicki's car is in the driveway, so I go around the side. Looking through the glass patio doors, I see Vicki on the couch, watching TV. It must be up loud, or else she's just spaced out like usual. I'm about to knock on the glass when I look over and spot Gran on the hill out back, in her garden. Perfect.

I'm halfway there when Jake's German shepherds show up on patrol duty, wearing the shock collars that zap them if they try to leave the grounds.

I slow but don't stop, hoping they recognize me. The dogs silently circle me, then come close for a sniff.

"Hi, guys. You know me. I'm family."

They always treat Squirrel as one of the pack. Me, I get long stares from their hungry eyes. Like if the command were given, they'd take me down. Right now they only keep pace with me, watching and waiting. So I keep moving.

When I reach the garden they hold back, keeping their eyes on me.

The path through the bushes is lined with wood chips. Gran hears my crunching footsteps and looks back, startled, as if she's been caught at something, or someone's come for her.

"Ty, honey! What are you doing here?"

"Brought you a little surprise."

I unzip my backpack and pull out the worn leather satchel I got from storage. Gran's eyes light up, and she undoes the clasp, opening the flap.

"My old tools! Look at that, they're all here."

The gardening kit has a variety of pruners, clippers, knives with curved blades and a small handsaw.

Gran reaches in and grabs a pair of shears. "See, they fit my big hands perfectly, like they did my mother's. I've missed all these."

"Yeah, I remembered you saying that, so I thought I'd dig them out of the basement." It feels good to see her happy. But she won't be so glad to see what else I've brought.

"Let me try them out."

I follow her to the hydrangea bushes, where she prunes the shriveled remains of last year's blooms.

"Still sharp after all these years," she says. "Thanks, honey."

"I found something else when I was looking. Here." I hand her a stuffed envelope. "Old photos."

She puts the shears away and sets the satchel down. "Let's see."

There were boxes of photos in the basement, sealed with yellowed tape like they hadn't been opened in decades. I selected a handful that I thought might be useful with Gran.

I watch her go through them, starting with shots of Dad and Jake when they were small.

"My boys. Look at Teddy. He grew so fast I couldn't keep up. His shirts were always too small, his pants too short. Nothing fit him for more than a week." She laughs at one photo of the boys wrestling in front of a TV showing real wrestlers in the ring. "They were like puppies. And there's Teddy in his team uniform back in junior high. He was made to play basketball. If only he hadn't wrecked that ankle."

Dad stands with the ball in one hand, holding it out to the camera like he's giving it up, with the same serious frown I'm used to. I wonder if this was taken before or after Lucy was killed.

The next picture is of Lucy. I slipped it in there, the shot from the yearbook cropped so it just shows her laughing and covering her mouth to hide that chipped tooth.

"Do you remember her?" I search Gran's face for any reaction. All I get is a blank look and a shake of the head.

"Doesn't look familiar." She checks the back of the photo to see if there's a note, then moves on.

Guess it was a long shot that she might give me the connection between Lucy and our family. Anyway, I shuffled the deck with these pictures, leading up to what comes next.

My grandfather. The Mad Dog, sitting on a motor-cycle, looking badass in black leather. Thick, wavy dark hair, three-day stubble and a wolfish grin. His eyes stare right out of the photo at me.

I look at Gran's face and feel a stab of guilt. I don't want to do this, but I have to. She seems to slouch a little, as if the day has suddenly gone cold around her.

The last picture shows them all together, with Gran and the boys kneeling by a Christmas tree and my grandfather standing behind them, his hands on Gran's shoulders. The three in front look frozen in his shadow, their smiles stiff and pained.

"How hard was he on the boys?" I ask.

It takes a moment before she finds her voice.

"That was such a long time ago," she says, as if those memories could have faded. Like she isn't haunted.

I know she doesn't want to talk about all that. Still, I can't leave it.

"But it got bad for my dad?"

Gran takes a deep breath and lets it out with a

shudder. "He was hardest on Teddy. My fault, really. Teddy would get in Doug's way when he came after me, took the hits meant for me. It made his father furious that any of us would stand up to him. And Teddy was so big, taller than Doug by the time he was eleven."

When you're so big so young, people think you can take more, that they can be rougher with you. I got that at school, everyone treating me like I was older.

There's no easy way to ask what else I need to know, so I just say it.

"I was talking to Celia back at the Zoo. She told me how Granddad was kind of popular with the women on the block."

I wince, putting that out there. Gran doesn't look surprised or hurt, though, just shakes her head a bit. "If you're asking did he run around on me, yes, I knew what he was up to. Never said anything to him about it. It was just the way he was."

"And do you think he was violent with them too?"

She shrugs. "It wouldn't shock me. He always had that blind rage. Anything could set him off."

"How far do you think he could go with it? I mean, were you scared he might ever . . . kill you?"

Gran looks down at the Christmas shot, hunched as if she can still feel those hands pressing on her shoulders.

"When it goes on for so long, when it's all you know, you go past scared, to numb. Just waiting for it to happen, for him to go too far. It might have come to that, if he hadn't died young himself."

"How *did* he die?"

"Stroke. That ran in his family."

I'd heard it was a stroke, but that doesn't fit with what Jake said when he was drunk. I can't stop now.

"Uncle Jake said how Dad never fought back, he just took it. But that he beat Granddad in the end. That he got him back. Had the last laugh."

That startles her and she meets my gaze. "He shouldn't have said that. Must have been drinking."

"He was. But, what did he mean? How did Dad *get* him?"

"Why so many questions, honey? And about such horrible things? Best left forgotten."

But nobody *has* forgotten. They're just not talking.

"Me and Dad have been having some troubles . . . working through some stuff. I'm trying to understand him better, the way he is. And trying to fix things. He won't say, but I think a lot of the problems we're going through have to do with what happened with Granddad. All that old, bad stuff. So can you tell me the truth about what went on back then? And what Jake meant?"

Gran shakes her head a little, glancing away. I look at her green eyes, the left one permanently damaged and darker, its pupil blown wide. When I was little I asked her why it was like that, and she said it was her "witchy" eye, good for seeing in the dark. Then she winked at me, getting me to giggle. It was only years later I found out from Mom that the Mad Dog did that to her.

For every question, she has some evasion.

Reaching out, I touch her hand gently, making her focus on me.

"It's important, Gran. I need to know."

I hold her gaze till she gives in with a shaky sigh.

"All right, Tyne. If it'll help fix things with you and your father. But, never tell."

"Never tell." It's our family motto.

"The truth is, Douglas was a beautiful, rotten, miserable man. I really think he was wired wrong in his head, more than just violent. Maybe that was what killed him. No other way to explain how he could be so charming, warm and funny one moment and so vicious and brutal the next. One time he told me, 'You really have to love something to hurt it so bad.'"

She looks at the photo in her hand.

"Anyway, the day it happened, me and Teddy were in the kitchen. I was making dinner when Doug got home. He was smiling, but that didn't mean anything. He smiled when he was happy and when he was raging mad. Someone had told him they ran into me at the bank. The thing is, Doug never let me do the banking, wouldn't even let me have any cards. The accounts were all in his name, and he gave me money to run the house. I tried to lie about being at the bank, said they must have seen someone else. But he already knew what I was up to. I'd been hiding money away, not much, but it wasn't safe to keep it around the apartment, so I opened my own account. And he knew what that meant. It was my runaway fund, my escape plan." She hugs her arms. "He usually left my face alone, didn't want what he did to show. So right then, in the kitchen, he punched me in the stomach. Knocked the wind out of me. But then Teddy got between us. Like he always did. I was yelling for Doug to stop. Teddy had his arms up to shield himself."

Gran has to slow down to catch her breath. "Then Doug just froze in the middle of throwing a punch. Stood there stiff, his face gone red, eyes bulging. And suddenly he dropped to the floor like he'd been shot, and started seizing, making these choking sounds before freezing up again. Teddy and I stood still, staring down at him. His face was all contorted, and I knew what was happening to him. So did Teddy, and he was reaching for the phone to call for help, when I grabbed his arm and held him back. Because if we waited and just left him there, it might all be *over.* I held on to Teddy, and when he looked at me I shook my head. So we waited and waited, with Doug staring up at us. The longest moments of my life. I never prayed so hard for anything as I did for him to stop breathing. And then he did."

She pauses to breathe herself.

"Then we sat down. I knew Doug was gone at last, but I wanted to be sure. It was a miracle. I've never felt guilty about that, but I know your dad does. It was a blessing for me and a curse for him. My poor Teddy. My fault. I don't know how, but I should have saved him from all that. That's where I'm guilty, in failing him."

Gran goes quiet. The sun's still out, but the afternoon has chilled around us.

"So there it is," she says finally. "How are you going to look at me now? What'll you see?"

I gaze into her eyes. Our features are so much alike, she's me plus fifty hard years.

"I still see you, Gran." I put my arm around her shoulders. "I see us."

WHEN ME AND Gran come in from the garden, we find Aunt Vicki still watching TV—some new mass shooting in the States, with the death toll at the bottom of the screen.

"Vicki, do you want to join us for a bite?" Gran asks her. "We're going to try some of your cherry pie."

Aunt Vicki looks up from the couch, where she's curled under a blanket.

"Some pie, yes. Let me get that for you."

I know she doesn't like people messing around in her kitchen. Aunt Vicki keeps the house pristine, and whenever we visit I feel like she decontaminates it after we leave. She practically follows Squirrel around with a Dustbuster when he's let loose.

Vicki serves us up her black cherry pie, with vanilla bean ice cream scooped into perfect snowballs. She likes to cook, even though she doesn't seem to eat, and her stuff is delicious. I devour my slice and get seconds. Gran's got a sweet tooth too, and keeps up with me while Vicki pecks at hers, watching in awe at our appetites.

"You're both so big and tall. Makes me feel like Alice in Wonderland, when she's shrunk down to an inch."

Soon as I'm finished, Aunt Vicki rinses off my plate and fork and quarantines them in the dishwasher. Then she wipes down the counter and starts washing her hands. As she scrubs away, I notice something on her left hand. She's taken off her wedding band and set it on the counter while she soaps up, and on her ring finger there's a strange mark. A scar.

It catches my eye, and my heart skips a beat. No, that can't be!

"What's that?" I say. "On your hand there."

Vicki turns off the water and towels her hands dry. She glances at her left hand.

"Oh, you mean this?" She rubs the mark with her thumb.

"Can I see?"

She holds her hand out to me. I lean in close. That's it! The dead girl's *brand*.

"Where did you get that?" I ask.

"Back when I was young and stupid. Jake gave me that, did it himself. He even made the little iron he used."

"The brand?"

"Yes. Jake made it for me. He said, 'You can take off a ring, but this is forever, means you belong to me.'

He was something of an artist back then, could make such beautiful things. And such ugly ones. Hurt like hell, like you wouldn't believe."

I can't believe what I'm hearing and seeing. But I catch a glimpse of the lettering on the other side of her finger.

"Don't know how he talked me into it. But he has a way . . . Said it was like a permanent valentine. That's what the design means."

"'Mine in life and death,'" I say.

"That's right. How did you know?"

I shake my head. "Must have seen it before."

It's Jake's work! And the murder—his work too?

I get a dizzying double vision of that message, on both living flesh and dead.

Vicki slips her wedding ring back on.

I feel like I'm going to puke up all that pie.

"Need some air," I say, heading out the patio doors.

Stepping into the sun, I try to catch my breath.

Jake. He was the one Lucy was going to run away with, who she was in love with. He marked her, so she belonged to him.

She was his. In life and death.

29

IT'S DARK BY the time I get back to the Zoo from Jake's house.

Mom's heading out to work the late shift. Busy night at the bar with both Raptors and Leafs games going on.

"Left you meatball subs in the fridge," she says, looking hot in a tight black blouse and black mini. *Short skirts mean big tips,* she always tells me. "Eat, girl, you need the protein. Get you back in game shape."

I nod, still stunned from my discovery earlier.

Dad's in the living room, watching TV with Squirrel.

"Goodnight, Squirrelly," Mom calls out. "Bye, honey."

Then she's out the door.

I stare around the kitchen, lost, as if I don't know where I am or what I'm doing anymore.

I text Stick: big bad news. meet me up top?

He shoots back: be there in 10.

I splash some cold water on my face, take the subs and some Coke, then go up top.

Leaving the door to the roof unlocked, I set everything down on the lawn chairs and take in the city. This place might be a dump, but it has a million-dollar view. The skyscrapers are all lit up and dazzling—*like Christmas trees,* I said when Dad took me up here at night for the first time. *A forest of them,* he told me. Seemed like magic then, and it still has its spell.

The cold wind brushes my hair back and fills my lungs. As the holiday break comes to an end, our break from winter weather is ending too. A deep freeze is on the way.

I hear Stick coming up.

"Hey, what's this? A picnic?"

"I've got food and news."

"I'm starving for both."

So we eat, and I talk. About what I found out, and what has to happen next. I leave out the stuff about how Mad Dog died. Like Gran said, *Never tell.* Because the only thing that matters is Lucy.

And Jake.

"So it's crazy Uncle Jake?" Stick says when I'm done. "Richie Rich with the monster house and the muscle car. The life of the party."

"I've heard how psychopaths can be real charming. They're good at faking the human thing."

He had me fooled. But I guess he learned from his father. We already knew about Jake's wild temper and drunken abusive ways, but this is so far beyond it's scary.

"How sure are we?" Stick asks.

"Ninety-nine point nine nine nine sure. And remember how he lied when I asked if he ever knew a girl from the Weeds named Lucy?"

Stick stops in the middle of licking tomato sauce off his fingers. "Damn, you better watch out! He's gotta know something's up now, with you asking about her after all these years. Watch your back."

"Why? What's he going to do?"

"Look what he's already done."

Hadn't thought of that. Jake must be wondering where I got Lucy's name. But he doesn't know that I found her body, and that I'm onto him.

"This explains why Lucy's foster sister got spooked when she heard your name was Greer. She was scared of Jake. Her old classmate said that Lucy was in love and going to run off with her mystery man. Jake was supposed to save her. So what went wrong?"

I take a deep breath. "There's only one way to find out. I have to confront my dad. Gotta make him talk. He can't deny it anymore, I've got too much proof."

Stick's shaking his head.

"What?" I say

"It's just . . . I'm getting a real bad feeling. This isn't going to end good for anybody."

"Well, there's no way out now. Never was. Not from the second I found her." I stare out over the forest of concrete Christmas trees. "Tomorrow I'll get

my dad alone, somewhere private, outside the apartment. He's the key to all this."

The night wind gusts between us with a touch of
frost. We wrap our arms around each other, sharing
a shiver.

30

MY DAY STARTS with the good hurt, bending, deep-stretching and massaging my knee.

Then I head to the pool to exercise. I text Stick to meet me for lunch first but get no reply. His response time is usually under ten seconds and he never passes on a chance to eat. Maybe Miss Diaz has him running chores.

Going for a long swim, I mentally zone out as I do my laps. But I can't stop thinking about my upcoming showdown with Dad. It'll hurt—and not the healing kind—but at least I'll finally know. Is he covering up for his brother or hiding his own role?

I shower off and walk home, texting Stick to touch base and help psych me up. He's still not answering. Maybe his phone is out of juice or out of whack, but it's not like him to be disconnected like this. When I call him it goes to voice mail.

Where are you? I keep trying.

Last I heard from him was his wake-up pic, showing

him with a huge lion roar-yawn, captioned *Dawn yawn of the dead*.

Since that, silence. Maybe his cell had a seizure or something.

Back at the Zoo I check Dad's "daily disaster" list to see where to find him, away from Mom and Squirrel. Looks like he's fixing a radiator leak on the tenth floor.

Mom's cleared some space in the living room where she's doing Pilates along with the show on TV. She looks at me upside down from between her legs. She keeps bugging me to try this stuff to improve my flexibility.

"Hey, Mom. Has Stick called or dropped by?"

"No. Haven't heard from him."

I leave her to her contortions.

In the hallway I have to step over the construction zone Squirrel has set up with bulldozers, dump trucks and Legos.

"Stick went for a ride," he says as I pass by.

Huh? He must have heard me asking Mom. "What was that?"

He makes a crashing sound, knocking over some blocks.

"What do you mean, Stick went for a ride?"

"In Uncle Jake's Mustang."

I look down at him. You always have to puzzle out what Squirrel says.

"Why do you say that?"

"'Cause I saw it. They were busting up the road

with jackhammers and filling the dump truck with rocks. Jake's Mustang was parked on the corner for a long time. It's fire-engine red. I like driving with Jake, he lets me sit up front."

"Were you watching the road crew working from the window today?" The view from up here is like TV for him. "And you saw Stick? You sure?"

"Stick left the Zoo and went in the street, and Jake was there. He got out of his car. Did you know a Mustang is the name of a horse? Remember I did the pony ride on Centre Island last year?"

"Squirrel, tell me what happened when Jake got out of his car."

"Jake got out and stopped Stick. They talked. Then he hugged him."

That doesn't sound right. "Jake hugged Stick?"

"Big hug. Then they got in the Mustang. He even let Stick drive. I want to drive."

"Stick was driving? You sure?"

"Sure. Jake hugged him into the car. Stick got behind the wheel and then they drove away."

I get a sick feeling as I try to picture that. Jake would never let anybody drive that car. Unless he forced Stick in. Maybe even had a gun on him. But that's crazy.

"You making this up? Or is it for real?"

"For real."

"When was this?"

Squirrel shrugs, no good with keeping time. I try another way.

"What did you have for lunch?"

Immediately he says, "Peanut butter and banana sandwich."

"And did you see Jake before or after your peanut butter and banana?"

"Before."

So it happened this morning, around the time Stick went silent.

What the hell is going on? I look out the window where Squirrel usually perches and watches, and focus on the corner where this would have gone down. Jake was waiting for Stick. But why? What's he want with him? Me asking about Lucy might have made him suspicious, even enough for him to come looking for me. But Stick? He had told me to watch my back, when he should have been watching his own.

I dial Stick again. It goes straight to voice mail. I text him: 911. Then: Call me NOW. I send both messages half a dozen times. This is bad—he's never, ever out of touch with me like this.

No reply. Dead quiet.

I call Miss Diaz. No luck. She says he's been gone all day.

Why would Jake take Stick? Does Jake somehow know that the body got uncovered after all these years? Did Dad tell him, when he moved and buried her? And then I came asking about Lucy? Could he have found out how me and Stick have been nosing around?

Shaking, I go to my room, redialing Stick every ten seconds, hanging up when it goes to voice mail.

It's four in the afternoon. Uncle Jake has had Stick for a long time. What do I do? How about if I call Jake? Let him know I know what's going on, so he better not try anything stupid.

Mom will have his numbers on her cell. As I'm leaving my room to go get hers, my phone rings. The screen says it's Stick. Finally!

"Stick, where are you? What the hell?"

"Hey, Tiny."

It's Jake. My heart seizes up.

"What are you doing with his phone?"

"What am I doing? I'm sending you a picture."

A message appears on my screen: This photo will auto-delete in 10 seconds. Then the image comes through.

I gasp. No. No. No.

It's Stick, but I can barely tell. His face is bloodied and bruised, the eyes so hideously swollen that they're squeezed to slits. Trails of blood run from his nostrils and he's got a fat lip, split and bleeding.

My heart pounds in my ears. Can't breathe. Can't—

Then the screen goes blank.

"Got that?" Jake asks.

"Stop! Just—just stop it! Don't hurt him!"

"Too late for that. Don't worry, he's still breathing."

"What—what do you want?"

"Heard what you've been up to. Digging into things better left buried. Bad idea, Tiny."

"You can let him go. He doesn't know anything."

"He knows too damn much."

"We'll keep quiet. Won't tell anybody."

Silence.

"I swear. Just let him go."

"I hear you've got something that belongs to me."

"What?"

"Use your brain, Tiny. I'm sure you can put your *finger* on it."

I glance at the desk drawer where I've got Lucy's finger.

"So," he says. "Let's do a trade. I get my property back, and you get your boy."

"Okay. Whatever you want."

"Bring it to me."

"Where?"

"You remember how to get to my salvage yard, out in Pickering?"

"Yeah."

"Be here in an hour."

"Okay. Okay. But let me talk to him."

"He's not up to chatting right now. Taking a nap. Here, listen."

Pressing my ear to the phone, I hear a low groan and ragged breathing.

"That's it, Tiny. Your proof. Now get moving, the hour's counting down. And don't try anything dumb. I'll be waiting."

Then he's gone. I stare at the empty screen. Stick looked half-dead, but he's still breathing.

Get moving! I dig the pill bottle with the gray finger out of my drawer. Glancing around the room, I think whether I should bring something more with me, some kind of weapon. But no—don't be dumb.

Just go! Gotta get there fast, need the keys to the truck.

Rushing down the hall, I run into Dad. He's digging in the supply closet in his stained overalls, his toolbox open on the floor. He looks up from sorting through his wrenches and sees my face.

"What's wrong?"

"Stick. Jake took Stick and beat him up. He—he's crazy. I can't talk. Gotta go."

"*What?* Wait. Slow down and tell me what's going on."

There's no time. But he's blocking me. So I just blurt it out.

"We found out about the dead girl. That body you took away. I know everything now. Me and Stick tracked her down and discovered who she was—Lucy Ramirez. Jake killed her! But he found out we were looking into it, and now he's taken Stick and beat him half to death. Jake's got him. And I'm gonna get him back."

I push past, hardly seeing Dad's stunned expression. I must have been shouting all that, because Mom's at the end of the hallway watching.

"What's with the yelling? And what's that about Stick?"

I shake my head. "Can't talk now."

"Hold on."

"No. I'm leaving."

She grabs my arm as I reach the kitchen. "Tell me."

I could shove her out of my way, but she's not going to let me go. So I give it to her quick, so fast I'm not even sure if I'm making sense. But I race through what's happened these past few days. Breathless, I get it all out in maybe a minute. Feels like forever.

She's looking at me like I'm nuts. Dad's behind me now. She snaps a few questions at him that I don't catch. My heartbeat is in my ears, deafening, screaming at me to run out of here. Go!

I make out scraps of what he's telling her: "Jake hid the body . . . I never knew she was there . . . panicked . . ."

I don't hear the rest, just see the confusion on Mom's face, the disbelief. But then she gets a strange look of recognition. And I realize what that expression must mean.

"Wait." I break in on them. "Mom, you knew?"

She shakes her head. "I just knew from long ago that your dad . . . cleaned up after Jake one time when he was a kid. I knew a girl died, but I never had any idea her body was . . . down there."

I can't believe what I'm hearing. "What? You knew Jake killed a girl?"

"No. That's not what happened. It wasn't like that. Tell her," she says to Dad.

"No!" I yell. "There's no time. Gotta go, or Stick's dead."

Dad reaches out to me, but I pull away.

"What does Jake want with Stick?" he asks. "Why is he holding him?"

"Because he wants to trade him to me."

"Trade him for what?"

"For this." I pull the bottle out of my pocket.

Mom squints at it. "What is *that*?"

"A finger. Her finger. It fell off in the chute when you moved the body."

Dad goes white.

"Oh my God." Mom's horrified.

Then another voice breaks in. Squirrel. "Hey, when's dinner? Can I have a cookie?"

We all turn to see him standing in the doorway holding a toy tank. If he heard anything we've been saying, it's not showing.

Mom rushes over and hustles him out. "We'll eat soon, honey. I'll bring you a snack, but let's go see what's on Animal Planet."

"Can I have Oreos?"

"Where is Stick now?" Dad says. "Where did Jake say to go?"

"The salvage yard."

Dad nods. "Give that finger to me. I'll do it and get Stick back."

"No. Jake said for me to bring it. Gave me an hour to get there."

He rubs his stubbled jaw, scowling. "Can't believe he's gone so far."

Mom comes back. The TV in the living room is turned up loud to cover our voices.

"Jake sent me a photo of what he's done to Stick.

He's hurt bad. Jake needs this thing, wants to get rid of it, I guess. Evidence of what he did."

"He's at the salvage yard," Dad tells Mom.

She takes the bottle from me and looks at the gray thing inside. "Okay, here's what has to happen. Tyne, you're not going anywhere. Your dad will go meet him."

I grab the bottle back. "No. It has to be me. I'm not risking Stick's life."

Mom tries to stare me down, but I'm not backing off.

"You both go, then," she says. "But he deals with Jake."

I give in. "Right, whatever. But let's go!"

She nods. We all rush to the elevator, where I pound the button and wait for it to come.

"Get this done," she tells Dad. "Get Stick back, and get the hell out of there. Then come home! Anything happens to her . . ." She doesn't have to say any more.

"Nothing's going to happen. I can handle Jake."

"No," she says. "You can't, and you never could. Tyne, you stay in the truck. If things go bad—don't think, just get out of there."

The elevator finally arrives. I rush in and jab the lobby button.

As the doors are closing Dad tells Mom, "I'll make this right. I'll fix it."

But it's too late for that.

Maybe too late for Stick.

31

"FASTER," I TELL Dad.

"I go any faster we'll get pulled over."

"How much longer?"

"Twenty minutes."

The sun's gone down and it's getting dark out, dropping below freezing.

The salvage yard is where Jake stores construction supplies and stuff from demolished buildings.

I've got the pill bottle in my hand, turning it over and over, wondering how everything got so bad, so fast. Stick had a bad feeling about where all this was headed. He was right.

"I'm sorry," Dad says. "I thought I'd convinced you that you were just seeing things."

"That I believed your lie?"

He swallows hard. "Yeah. I just— I thought it was the only way to get you to put it behind you. Never guessed that you'd kept looking. There seemed no other way out."

"How about the truth?"

"How could I tell you? What could I say that wouldn't open the whole rotten thing up? I couldn't ask you to keep that secret. I didn't want to make you part of it, for it to touch you."

"How could you . . ." It's impossible to find the words, to ask for answers I really don't want to hear. But I have to try. "How could you be part of it, of what happened to that girl?"

"It was an accident. All of it."

"An accident? I saw the body. She was butchered."

"It's not how it looks."

"What!"

"It wasn't murder. Not really."

In the dark interior of the truck I try to read his face in the shadows. He sounds like he's choking on his words.

"How did you get mixed up in it?" I ask.

He takes a shaky breath. "I was only supposed to be a lookout. This was twenty-five years ago. I was fourteen. Jake said he needed my help. He was in trouble and wanted me to guard one of the storage rooms in the basement, make sure nobody came near it. He was caught up in something bad. I didn't know what he was hiding. He told me not to look, to just wait in the hall and guard the door while he ran to get something. Said he'd only be twenty minutes."

I stare straight ahead, needing to find out the truth, but wanting to be at the yard already. Getting Stick is all that matters.

"When I was waiting for Jake, I heard moaning coming from the room. I was scared to death. Didn't know what to do. I called through the door, 'You okay in there?' Nobody answered. The moaning got louder. Then there was a scream that cut right through me. There was a girl inside, and something was really wrong. I had to look. So I used the master key to open the door."

Dad guns the engine to make the next light and we fly through an intersection.

"There was a girl. I knew her from the neighborhood. She was lying on a piece of foam on the floor, shrieking in pain, shaking and soaked with sweat. Her eyes were wide open and staring at me. But she couldn't speak without screaming. I told her I'd get help. I was running for the elevator when Jake came rushing back. I said to call an ambulance, but he told me no. She was overdosing, and he'd got the meds he needed to help her. When we got to the room it was too late. She was already seizing. Too far gone. Right then, she stopped shaking and went stiff, stopped breathing, stopped everything. I got down and started pumping her chest, trying CPR, blowing into her mouth. I tried, really. But she was gone."

I'm shaking my head, trying to keep up with Dad. "No. She couldn't have died that way. I saw how she was, her body cut open."

Dad tries to clear his throat. "Jake did that after. When she was already dead."

"What? Why?"

"Because . . . he had to get the drugs out of her."

"What?"

"The girl, she was a mule. She was carrying a shipment of cocaine inside her. She'd just got off a plane from Mexico, on a drug run."

I stare at him as we speed through the streets.

"Jake was a dealer?"

"No, but he worked for one. Jake was a recruiter. He found the girls and taught them to be mules to carry the drugs. The girl would fly down to Mexico with a handler who posed as her aunt, pretending they were on vacation. And before they flew back to Toronto she'd swallow a bunch of condoms filled with cocaine."

"She was a mule?"

"Jake convinced the girls it was easy money. When they got back from a run, he'd pick them up at the airport, after they cleared customs, and deliver them to the dealer's doctor, where they'd get the drugs safely out of them. It had always worked okay."

"So how . . . how did she end up at the Zoo?"

"Things got screwed up. The dealer's place was raided, so Jake had nowhere to deliver the girl. The handler was only paid to get her past customs. After that, she gave her over to Jake. He had to find somewhere private and secure so the girl could pass the drugs out of her system. The Zoo had all those empty rooms where nobody ever went, and we had the keys. So he brought her there."

"What went wrong?"

"Everything. Jake had never done more than sell

the girls on it and drive them to the dealer to get the shipment taken out of them. But time is a big factor. You can't leave the condoms inside too long, because they might break, or get damaged by stomach acids. That can be deadly. You can OD. When you swallow the drugs, they give you something to make you constipated so you don't pass the drugs before you get to your destination. But the handler gave the girl too much of that stuff, and then the flight was delayed. When Jake left me to guard the room, he was going for laxatives, trying to save her. But one of the condoms burst. She never had a chance."

Dad's breathing hard, caught in the memory.

I don't want to hear any more, but I have to. "And after?"

"After that he . . . got the drugs out. Said if he didn't get the coke to the dealer, he'd be dead too. I—I waited outside. Just sat on the floor, heaving. When he was done, he called me back in. It was . . . unbelievable, horrific. I puked till there was nothing left in me. Jake said he'd take care of the body, and told me to clean up the blood. I said I couldn't do it. Then he said we were in this together now, both of us." Dad wipes the sweat from his forehead. "So I cleaned it up."

I check the time on my cell. "Dad! We've got five minutes. Almost there?"

"We'll make it."

I'm sick at what he told me, but more frantic for Stick.

Dad keeps going. "I'm sorry. So sorry. Back then

I was scared, stupid and fourteen. Didn't know what else to do. And I never knew what Jake did with the body. Not till you found her."

"Why did you go and bury her?"

We turn off the main road into an industrial area. It's fully dark now.

He shakes his head. "I panicked. If the cops found out, that would be *it*. I'd lose everything. You, Mom, Squirrel. I was trying to protect us. Thought I could make it go away. I couldn't ask you to live with knowing what I'd done back then. So I lied. Tried to make you think you were seeing things. But I was wrong, about everything."

"And now Jake wants the finger back, to get rid of the evidence. But there's still her body buried out in the woods."

Dad shakes his head. "After I buried it, I called him and we fought about it. How could he dump her in the wall like that? He wanted to know where I'd put her. And I told him. So he's got her body."

I look down at the pill bottle. "He just needs this."

Dad hits the brakes in front of a tall chain-link gate topped with barbed wire.

We're here.

32

IN THE GLARE of our headlights Dad runs up to the gate. There's a guardhouse trailer on the other side, but nobody in sight. The yard is lit by floodlights on tall poles around the perimeter. Most of the place lies in shadow. Dad reaches out and pulls the gate back. Somewhere beyond, Jake's got Stick.

As I watch Dad, I catch something moving from behind the trailer. Two low figures jump out toward him. No time to shout a warning before the silence is broken by angry barking. Big dogs rush Dad, but they're pulled up short by their chains.

Dad comes back. "He knows we're here now."

"Any more dogs inside?"

"Don't think so."

He pulls the truck through. Leaving the gate open, we cruise the yard. The place is huge, with towering stacks of lumber and shipping containers forming dark corridors. We pass piles of bent girders and pipes heaped into hills of twisted metal.

Where are you, Stick?

We turn a corner into at a dead end lit by the high beams of a car. Jake's Mustang.

Dad pulls to a stop about twenty feet from it. When he cuts the engine the night goes quiet. Even the dogs quit howling.

Squinting against the headlights, I make out a lone figure slumped in the Mustang's passenger seat. I see curly spiked hair.

"Stick!" I reach for the door, but Dad holds me back.

"No, Tyne. Listen, you stay here. Let me do this."

He gets out and steps away from the truck.

I crack open my door and climb out too. Can't sit and wait with Stick so close. I hold up one hand, shielding my eyes from the beams, desperately willing Stick to *move. Look up.*

But the only movement comes from the shadows behind the car.

"We've got a family reunion," Jake says, breath steaming in the frozen air. He's keeping his distance.

Dad steps in front of the truck. "What have you done?"

"What we do best, bro. Fix and clean."

He's drunk. That's not good.

"Give me the kid," Dad says. "He never did anything."

Jake leans on his car. "He went dragging out what should've been left alone. Him and your girl. Hey, Tiny."

"It's over now," Dad tells him.

"Not for me."

Dad takes two steps toward the Mustang and Jake pushes off from it.

"Hold on, Teddy."

Jake's holding something in his right hand.

"Dad! He's got a gun!"

"Listen to her, bro. Don't be stupid. Let's trade. You've got something that belongs to me."

I hold the plastic bottle up. "Here it is."

"Toss it over, Tiny."

I throw it to him and the bottle lands at his feet. He picks it up, goes to the front of his car and bends, holding the bottle up to the headlights, while leaning his gun hand on the hood.

"That's my mark," he says. "She never made a sound when I branded her. She was tough, my little Lucy. You think I'm some kind of monster for what I did. But I tried to save her."

"She was just a kid, Jake."

"She knew what she was getting into. Her dying, that's not on me."

"Give us the boy."

Jake has to steady himself on the hood. Drunker than I thought. Stuffing the bottle in his pocket, he goes to the passenger side and taps on the window with the gun barrel.

I hold my breath. *Stick. Move! Let's go.* Stick doesn't even twitch.

Jake opens the door and nudges him. "Out."

Finally, Stick flinches. And I can breathe again.

"Out, kid. Go."

Stick slides slowly out of the car, grabbing on to the roof to pull himself up.

I start forward.

"Wait," Dad tells me as Jake turns the gun in my direction.

But I can't wait. Stick staggers to the front of the Mustang, barely keeping on his feet.

"Easy, Tiny," Jake warns.

I get there just as Stick starts to fall, and catch him. I stand frozen, shocked. The swelling has deformed his face, with one eye squeezed shut. Dried blood is crusted all over, his nose a lump. Skin bruised dark purple. His good eye focuses on me.

"Ty," he wheezes. "Came for me."

"I got you now." I force the words past the choke in my throat.

Then he sags against me and I half carry him toward the truck.

"Jake, what did you do?" Dad sees Stick's mutilated face.

"What I had to. Kid had it coming, poking in my business. Not gonna let anybody try and take me down. I fought too hard to get what I've got."

"We're over, Jake. I never want to see you again, or hear from you."

"Whatever you say. Once I get rid of this"—he holds up the bottle—"there's nothing to worry about. Nothing left to show of her. But make sure your girl keeps her mouth shut. Or else."

Dad was turning to leave, but that stops him. "No," he says, his voice a low growl.

"No what, Teddy?"

"You don't threaten her. Don't you ever."

"Hey, Tiny stays quiet, she's got nothing to worry about."

"You don't come anywhere near her. Never."

"Just make her understand. So she won't get hurt."

I reach the truck with Stick as Dad closes in on Jake.

"Dad, no!" My shout echoes.

The dogs at the gate start barking and howling.

"Don't be dumb, Teddy. We both know you don't got it in you. The old man beat the fight out of you. Tiny's safe as long as she stays silent."

But Dad keeps going, even as Jake raises the gun.

My heart thunders.

And then everything goes slow motion on me—Jake, gun pointed at Dad as he rushes forward, the dogs raging and snarling so loud, like they've broken free and are racing toward us, while I open my mouth for a last scream—

Then time snaps forward.

Dad chops down on Jake's gun hand as he crashes into him. The gun doesn't fire, but falls to the side. Dad tackles him onto his car.

Dad's way bigger, but Jake has his legs up to kick him off. They roll on the hood. Jake gets him in a headlock. But then Dad rises up and brings his weight down, crushing Jake with an impact that rocks the car and breaks his hold.

Dad starts beating on him. Wild punches, fists swinging, elbows hammering down. Jake tries to shield himself, arms raised to block.

Dad never fought back before, but it's exploding out of him now. Jake's head bangs off the hood again and again, till he can't keep his arms up and goes limp.

"Stop!" I scream. But Dad's way past hearing me.

I've got to break it up before he kills Jake. But Stick's hanging on to me. I lean down until he's sitting on the truck's bumper and then race over.

I've pulled girls out of scraps on the court. But Dad's heavier than me. Raging blind. Got to get him off.

So I jump him from behind, knocking him off-balance. We slide across the hood. He tries to shake me, but I grab on tight and bear-hug him, trying to heave him backward. For a second I get his feet off the ground, and we crash to the gravel.

We roll away from each other, gasping. The anger in his eyes gives way as he sees me.

"You okay?" he pants.

"Yeah. You?"

He nods.

We stand up.

Jake sprawls motionless on the hood of the car. With his arms and legs bent at awkward angles, he looks like he's fallen from a high place, his impact denting the hood. His face is bloody. Can't even tell if he's breathing, he's so still.

We wait for a long minute.

Then a shudder runs through his limp body. Coughing, wet and harsh, turns into a strange choking sound. It goes on and on—but he's not choking.

He's laughing.

Rolling on his side, he spits out a mouthful of blood. And keeps on laughing.

"Teddy," he wheezes. "You got the Mad Dog in you after all. Feels good, right? Letting it out."

Dad shakes his head. "We're done."

Then he turns to the truck and I follow him. I gently lift Stick from his crouch on the bumper.

"It's in our blood, Teddy," Jake calls after Dad. "We're mad dogs."

I ease Stick into the truck so he can lie down with his head in my lap.

We back out. Frozen in our lights, Jake is propped up on one elbow, his face a bloody mask, laughing. We speed out of there.

"Hospital," I tell Dad.

Looking at Stick, I want to cry. "Hang in there. We'll get you help. Fix you up. Where's it hurt?"

Dumb question, I know. He whispers, "Everywhere."

"I'm so sorry." I brush my hand over his curls, stiff with dried blood and dirt.

"S'okay," he mumbles. "Not my first beatin'. Just . . . worst." And he breaks my heart by trying to smile. "Tell 'em . . . say I got jumped . . . or mugged."

Even now, his brain's still firing, working up a cover story for this mess.

"You saved me. My girl."

"Shhh, now. Just breathe. Keep breathing."

Even though we're speeding through the night, it seems to take forever, but it can't be more than fifteen minutes before we're pulling up to the emergency loading zone at the hospital.

Stick's passed out by then. I pull him out of the truck and hold him up. Dad comes around to help me.

"I'll take him," he says.

"No. You can't come in. Look at you. They'll think you did this."

Dad glances down at himself and sees his shirt torn, dirty and dusty, the bloody mess of his fists, all scratched and cut up. He looks at his hands like they belong to somebody else.

"Just go home."

"Home?" He sounds confused. As if he's forgotten the way.

"Mom's waiting. Tell her . . . tell her we're safe."

"Safe." He nods. "Okay."

I leave him there, and carry Stick inside. He's a skinny guy, only right now he's dead weight, arms and legs hanging.

But I'm a giant. I could carry him for miles. As I step into the bright lights of the hospital, he lets out a whimper like a scared, lost thing.

"It's all right. I've got you."

33

AFTER I HAND Stick over to the emergency room staff, I text Mom that it's over and we're all okay. Meaning everybody's still breathing—I'll let Dad fill in the details. Then I make the call to Miss Diaz to let her know about Stick. She doesn't panic, just cuts right to it—how bad is the damage, where is he, and she's on the way.

While I'm waiting to hear about his condition, I give them his name and info, with his cover story— how he got jumped, mugged and beaten. I'm standing by the ER desk, holding a clipboard with a medical history form I'm supposed to be filling out for Stick, losing track of time and staring off in the direction they took him, when I feel a hand on my shoulder.

It's Vega, looking pissed. She gives me her laser stare.

"Where is he?"

"Down that hall."

Miss Diaz is right behind her. She goes up to the desk and knocks on it to get the attention of the nurse.

"You've got my boy here. Skinny Latino. Name's Ricky. Big girl brought him in. I want to see him. Now."

You don't say no to Miss D. You can try, but she's going to get her way. They take her and Vega back, with me trailing.

When the nurse pulls back the curtain we see Stick with an IV in his arm, oxygen tubes in his nose and wires hooked up to a heart monitor. If it wasn't for his spiky curls he'd be unrecognizable. His features are all distorted and bruised. My legs get shaky, but Miss Diaz doesn't even pause. She takes his hand, feels his pulse, leans in close to hear him breathe, then whispers in his ear.

"Sleep easy, Ricky. Mama D's here."

I watch his heart on the monitor like I'm watching my own, matching his beat for beat, echoing him.

Later, they take him to another room. The X-rays show a fracture of the left orbital bone, at the eye socket, but his nose isn't broken. They stitch up some head cuts and pull a knocked-out tooth from under his tongue, but the rest of him is intact.

"Looks worse than it is," the doc tells us. Easy for him to say.

I'm not ready when the police come. All I've told Miss D is the basic bull Stick came up with. But with the two cops in the room questioning me, all I can say is we got jumped and fought back. I can't tell why I'm not hurt, why the blood on me isn't mine.

"Where did this happen?" one cop asks.

"Not sure. We were out walking."

"What did the attackers look like?"

"Don't know, it was so dark. There were two big guys."

It's not going good, and I'm starting to stumble over my words. But then Vega saves me.

"That's all we got to say," she tells them.

"We're going to need more," one cop insists. "We have to file a report."

"You do what you gotta do. But she's done talking."

"That's not going to work. She's—"

"She's a minor," Miss D breaks in. "Seventeen. So you can't question her without a parent present."

She knows the drill.

The cops take my contact info, say they'll be in touch.

When they're gone, Miss D starts to set up house in Stick's room, making it clear she's not leaving till he does. From her big, bottomless bag, she takes out a comforter and spreads it over the thin hospital blanket to keep Stick warm. On the little bedside table she lays out a thermos, a box of tissues, her cheese Goldfish crackers, the pocket-sized Bible she always carries with her, and a fat romance novel, along with her tablet and earplugs. She must have an emergency kit ready to go. Who knows how many times, for how many kids, she's done this. But still, I think Stick's special to her. Maybe because she's had him so long. Or just 'cause he's Stick. She settles in to a chair beside the bed.

Vega nudges me. "Walk with me, Stretch."

I follow her out to the parking lot, where we lean against her car. The night's freeze wakes me from the daze I've been in.

"Give it up," she says. "Let's hear it."

I don't know what to tell her.

"No lies," Vega warns me. "Feed me crap and I'll know it."

I take a deep breath. "Long story."

"I don't need all the details. Just give me the bullet."

So I do. How we got here has a lot of twists, but I don't hold back, knowing I can trust her.

Vega doesn't interrupt, shows no reaction.

By the end I'm breathless and drained.

She stands silent, arms crossed, staring at me long and hard. There's an electric shiver in the air between us—a vibe of violence, not aimed at me but I can feel it. Vega, the human razor blade.

"So," I say. "What are you gonna do?"

Her eyes are so cold they burn. "Me? I look like a cop to you?"

Then she pushes off from the car and heads back into the hospital. We find Miss Diaz sitting with her earplugs in, reading her romance. Stick's sleeping deep.

"Go home, Stretch. Come back in the morning."

I start to shake my head.

"Go. I'll be watching him. We're here. He's got family."

She's right. I'm no use right now, ready to collapse.

I lean in close to kiss Stick's ear, maybe the only part of him that's not hurting, and whisper, "Love you."

Then I leave, texting Mom that I'm coming home.

Pick you up? she asks.

No. Be there soon.

I need to be alone awhile. So I catch the subway. When I grab a seat, I notice two other passengers move away from me. Probably because of the blood on the front of my hoodie, with dirt and dust from the yard.

Stick's blood, and maybe some from Dad's ragged knuckles mixed with Jake's. I can still hear him. Shouting, *It's in our blood.*

Bad blood. Jake's a monster. But what is Dad? A liar, an accessory, a conspirator, or a victim himself? Maybe all those things.

All I know is I'm not ready to face him.

Mom's waiting in front of the Zoo. She looks up at me with a fierce scowl of love and worry, then puts her arm around my waist so I can lean on her, and takes me inside.

In the apartment, I pass by Dad. I don't meet his eye, just see his hands bandaged around the knuckles— Mom's work. She leads me straight to the bathroom.

"Sit." She pats the edge of the tub.

I do, and she pulls the hoodie off over my head. Like when I was a kid coming home muddy, she takes care of me now. I sit while she runs hot water in the sink, washing the blood and dirt from my hands. Back then, she'd scrub my small hands clean, but now hers look like a kid's soaping mine.

After toweling my hands dry, she takes a damp cloth to my face. It comes away filthy with dirt and blood. She searches for cuts or scrapes, but I'm all right.

"Bed," she says.

I nod, with her warm palms on my cheeks. We stay like that for a long moment as she stares deep in my eyes, searching for injuries hidden and invisible. Knowing where it hurts.

"Honey, your dad's a good man. Who did some wrong things." She sighs. "I can live with that. Can you?"

34

AFTER SUCH A wild, violent night I expected more of an explosion to follow. Sirens, cops at the door, screaming arguments around the house, thunder and lightning.

But there's only the calm after the storm. I wake to quiet.

Break's over and it's the first day back to school, but there's no way I'm going.

Before I head to the hospital, Mom makes me eat some eggs and toast. Then she takes Squirrel to school, while Dad's off doing odd jobs around the building.

Just another day, like last night never happened.

At the hospital I'm thrilled to find Stick awake and drinking a chocolate milk shake that Vega smuggled in. He won't be eating solids for a while.

He's propped up in bed with Miss Diaz holding the straw for him. The swelling has gone down a bit, but the bruising is even darker. The doctor's final verdict was no major broken bones or cracked ribs, some stitches here and there, and a little blood in his urine from a bruised kidney, but that's already clearing up.

I tell Miss Diaz I'll be staying for a while if she wants to take a break. She reluctantly agrees, heading home for a change of clothes, a bite and maybe a nap.

When she's gone I pull the chair in close.

"What I miss?" Stick mumbles. "How did it end?"

His eyes are slitted, but he's alert. So I fill him in on everything, from Squirrel spotting him being taken to when I got the picture Jake sent, Dad giving me the truth behind Lucy's death and his fight with Jake.

When I'm done, Stick drinks some water and slowly gives me his side of what went down after Jake grabbed him at gunpoint. Stick tried lying, telling him he had no idea what he was talking about. But Jake already knew. Dad had told him about finding the body and moving it, and when I asked him about a girl named Lucy he knew something was up. By the time Jake got Stick to the salvage yard, he was drunk and talkative, telling him how he'd poked around online, finding Stick's Facebook page and the tracing of the brand he'd posted asking for help with deciphering it. Stick tried to hold out, but Jake beat it all out of him, everything. Even how we talked to Lucy's foster sister, Rosie. Jake said some stuff that made Stick think Rosie might have been another one of his mules, which is why she was so scared when we showed up asking questions.

"He even told me he loved Lucy," Stick says.

I remember when Lucy's old school friend shared her suspicions with us that the guy Lucy had fallen for back then was abusing her, leaving her bruised and battered.

"Jake never loved anybody but himself. Never touched anything he didn't hurt."

Even after Stick had given up everything he knew, Jake kept beating on him till he was sure there was no more.

"Thought he was gonna kill me," Stick says. "He took my picture. Said, 'Smile for Tiny.'"

I shake my head. All those times growing up that I stood towering beside Stick as his unofficial body-guard, scaring off the bullies who had him in their sights, but when he needed me most, I wasn't there.

"I'm so sorry I dragged you into this mess," I tell him. "Almost got you dead. And for what?"

"It's not like the movies. When it's for real, some-times the bad guy wins."

I start to cry. Can't help it. He reaches for my face but doesn't have the strength to lift his arm. I take his hand, cool to the touch, and press it between my palms to warm him up.

"Don't worry, Ty. I'll live. You know how it is, some sticks break and some just bend. Like me."

I sniffle. He's a wreck, and he's trying to make *me* feel better. "Can I get you anything?"

"Nah. But how about you play naughty nurse? Give me a sponge bath, with a happy ending." His mouth twitches with a small smile.

I laugh. "Don't think you're up to it."

"I'm always up for it," he says sleepily.

But his eyes are sliding shut, and soon he's snoring softly. I cover him with his comforter and listen to him breathe. It's a good sound.

Maybe the bad guy won. But all that matters is I've got him. My bent Stick.

35

I DON'T KNOW how to talk to Dad anymore, how to be with him. Now it isn't lies keeping us apart, it's the truth of what he did, and why. Even though I get his reasons for cleaning up his brother's mess and hiding from his own guilt afterward. And all these years later with Lucy's body turning up, how he had to protect the life he'd made for himself. And guard his family.

I don't really feel like he's a stranger. I know who he is. I just don't know who *we* are, together.

So I keep my distance. Not hard with him working overtime on the Zoo's cracked foundation. That's what Dad was fighting about with Slimy the day he came here. Slimy wanted to do some cheap patchwork to hide the damage, but Dad said it was too dangerous to cover up.

I used to wonder why Dad never escaped the Zoo. With his wrecked ankle killing any college basketball dreams, and so beaten down by his father, I guess he couldn't see a way out. When Mad Dog died he took over as super to take care of his mother, and he just got stuck here.

Anyway, my focus now is on two things—Stick getting better, and my game. I'm only home to eat and sleep; the rest of the time I'm in school, at the gym or hanging with Stick at his place. No more slacking with my workouts. I do endless laps in the pool to get my lungs and endurance back, practice with the team to regain my rhythm. Because this is it! My senior year, my final season and my last chance to show the college scouts what Big Meat can do.

Two girls at Queen's Cross are already signed and committed to schools. I need to hustle. It's now or never.

After a week on a liquid diet—mostly milk shakes, pudding and ice cream—Stick can chew again. The only permanent damage is a missing molar. The swelling goes down and the bruises fade, so he's my Stick again. Only different. It's like he gets lost in his head sometimes, where I'll be talking to him and he'll be just *gone*. He's slower to smile, and scares easy. Jumpy as hell. A door slams and to him it's like a gunshot. I catch him looking behind him, on constant guard, watching his back. Can't blame him. I try telling him he's safe now. Jake's a psycho and a drunk, but he's not stupid. Too many of us know the truth for him to try anything. And he got what he wanted—the evidence of his crime—so there's nothing to connect him to some disappeared dead girl the world's already forgotten. It's over.

But not for Stick. He's haunted by nightmares, and all I can do is be there for him through the panic attacks. I talk him down, calming and distracting him. Getting him to breathe.

He doesn't blame Dad, the way I do. Dad's the closest thing he's ever had to a father. Stick's been talking to him a lot more than I have these past weeks.

When the cops try to follow up on the assault report, they have to deal with Mom. She speaks for me, telling them nothing. In basketball it's called "setting a screen," where your teammate keeps your opponent from getting to you. With Stick not talking to them either and nobody pushing to file a report, they drop it.

On the hard court, back in the game, I'm on a mission. Blocking and rebounding, fighting for the ball. A defense machine. Protecting my girls.

Stick cheers me on from the stands, and Mom brings Squirrel to the games when she's not working the night shift. What's missing is Dad. He's been to every game I ever played. But now he stays away. Mom says it's because he thinks I don't want him there. He doesn't want to distract.

Maybe he's right. I don't know. All I do know is that even when the stands are full, there's an empty place.

My knee still hurts, but the doc tells me it's healing fine. I lost some muscle when I was sidelined, and now that I'm back in beast workout mode, I have to eat like one.

Right now, it's dinner and I'm making bottomless bowls of spaghetti and meatballs disappear.

We all still eat together, Mom makes sure of that.

Even with me and Dad not talking, like we're invisible to each other across the kitchen table. Squirrel saves us from our silence with his nonstop commentary, everything that pops into his head.

"You're gonna explode," he says, watching me feast with shock and awe.

"Nah. I could eat a mountain of meatballs."

"I saw a guy eat sixty-eight hot dogs in ten minutes on TV. And he won, like, the eating Olympics. Bet you could beat his record."

"I could eat a hundred hot dogs, and still have room for a squirrel."

I lunge like I'm going to take a bite out of him. He ducks me, squealing with laughter.

Mom shakes her head. "My kid the cannibal. Where did I go wrong?"

The phone rings.

Dad gets up to answer it. The super's always on duty.

"Hello. *What?* Wait. Slow down. What's wrong?" He listens for a while, leaning on the counter, head down. "My God, you sure? How did . . ."

It sounds like a major disaster. Me and Mom exchange a look.

"Okay. I'm coming. I'm on my way." After hanging up, Dad just stands there, staring at the phone.

"What is it?" Mom asks.

He looks stunned. Takes him a moment to answer. "It's Jake."

"What does he want?" she says.

"I mean, that was about Jake. He's . . . he's dead."

36

KIDS DON'T GET death.

After all those nature shows Squirrel's seen, with the hunting and killing, blood and gore, you'd think he'd understand what it means. But I guess for him that's all TV stuff.

At the funeral, he kept asking me,

"Uncle Jake's in the box?"

"Yeah."

"He holding his breath?"

"No."

"Sleeping?"

"No."

"He coming back?"

I shook my head, putting my arm around him.

A good-sized crowd showed up for the funeral, mostly people connected with Jake's business.

Why was I there? Why even go? It's cold to say, but I came to see him gone. In the ground. It's like how Gran keeps Mad Dog's ashes—to be sure it's all over, that he's not coming back. So I can tell Stick he doesn't have to feel scared and hunted anymore. Maybe it won't end his nightmares, but he can rest easier.

They're calling Jake's death a freak accident. It happened on Highway 401 outside Toronto. He was driving to work in the city during the morning rush hour. Witnesses say the scene was horrific.

Smoke started pouring out from under the hood of his Mustang. Jake pulled off onto the shoulder. Before he could even stop, flames burst from the engine. And he couldn't get out. People saw him struggling to get the door open, but it must have jammed. Whatever went wrong, it went bad fast. The fire spread from the engine to the interior. The windows were sealed tight and bystanders said he was frantically trying to kick out the windshield as the car filled with black smoke and flames.

I saw the TV news report showing the incinerated frame of the Mustang, the tires melted to lumps of black rubber. A trucker who witnessed it all looked shaken.

"Can't get the screams out of my head," the man said. "He took a long time dying."

Investigators are going over the wreckage to determine the cause of the fire. But I don't know how they're going to find out anything. It looks like a bomb exploded. Jake had customized the engine of his muscle car, built it himself, so who knows what fatal mistake he made in the design.

But I'm not buying that it's an accident.

It's just too convenient. Too coincidental that some kind of brutal justice would fall on Jake after his crimes were revealed.

Because the universe doesn't work that way. There is no karma, no cosmic payback to punish the guilty. People get away with horrible things all the time. Bad guys win.

So, what am I thinking? I'm thinking, *Vega*.

I saw the scary cold look in her eyes at the hospital. I knew right then that this wasn't the end of it for her.

Vega, the ghetto rat. The razor blade. The mechanic.

When Stick was getting bullied she said, *Don't be the hunted, be the hunter.* She can take an engine apart blindfolded. And she'd had her eye on Jake's red Mustang before, when he came to see us at the Zoo.

The "accident" was perfect. Even if they somehow managed to pull something suspicious out of the wreckage, they'd never look at Vega. Jake and Vega were strangers. No link. No motive. Nobody would ever guess.

After the burial, we head back to Jake's house in Richmond Hill.

It's a cold, crisp day, with gray skies. Smells like snow on the way. Winter came late, but now it's got us in its teeth.

I watch as Squirrel rolls around on the ground with the dogs, their breath clouding in the air.

"Can I go on the trampoline?" he asks, grass-stained and breathless.

"Not today," I say.

There's a small gathering inside the house. So many people, and none of them knew what Jake really was.

But Vicki did. She lived with his temper and drunken rages, a prisoner in her own home. Branded like Lucy. His possession.

Should I be more shocked and horrified by Jake's gruesome death? Before this nightmare started, he was my loud, crazy, joking uncle.

Was it all a lie? Was he a total faker, a psycho without a soul? I remember Lucy's friend from school saying how she was showing signs of abuse, bruised and battered, before she disappeared. Was Jake hurting her? Who knows? All I feel is relief. He's gone. We're safe, and he's buried along with his crimes and secrets. Like what he did with Lucy's body. Wherever she is now, I hope he left her wrapped in my old blanket with the sunflowers. Something warm.

When I was talking with Stick before the funeral, he just shook his head at the whole thing.

"What was the moral of this story?" he asked me.

"If you're looking for morals, you came to the wrong place," I told him. "All I know is *his* story is done."

Dad walks up, bringing a juice box and a sandwich for Squirrel, and some dog treats for the German shepherds.

"Let me feed them," Squirrel says. "I want to do Uncle Jake's trick."

He gets the dogs to sit while he places a biscuit on

top of each one's nose. "Stay," he tells them. "Stay. And—go!" At the clap of his hands, the dogs snap their treats out of the air.

"There's lots of food inside," Dad says to me. "If you're hungry."

I nod. He doesn't seem to have any suspicions about how Jake died. For him it's just a strange, sudden shock.

"How's Gran taking it?" I ask.

Dad looks off to where she's standing, alone in her bare winter garden on the hill in the huge backyard.

"Hard to tell. She keeps it all inside."

Sounds familiar. Everything locked away, hidden and secret. Unspoken, but unforgotten.

I go to her now.

The garden is sleeping through the deep freeze. I find Gran crouched by a freshly dug hole. She's dressed in all gray, charcoal funeral dress and heavy coat against the wind chill, her silver hair pulled back in a knot.

She glances up. "Look at this. Those damn dogs are at it again, making a mess. Chewing up my tulip bulbs. They dig holes everywhere and bury things— toys, balls, the birds they kill. Never liked them. They're here to guard us, Jake said. But they never make me feel safe, with their hungry eyes watching. We should get rid of them now. Don't trust those dogs without Jake around to control them."

Gran reaches out a hand for me to help her up. She shakes her head at her tulip bed.

"Never liked that car either." She brushes dirt

from her fingers. "Too fast and flashy. But that's how he was. Teddy was always more like me. Gentle."

She should have seen him in the salvage yard that night. Blind with rage. She wouldn't have recognized him.

"But you're something else, Tyne. Not like us, something new. I've seen the way you play, nothing gentle there. Nobody pushes you around. You don't give in, don't back down."

"I can't. If I do, they win. That's how the game's played."

"It's more than the game. It's how you are." She takes my arm and leads me down the path. "Let me show you something else that's new. My creepers."

Gran brings me to the gardening shed. She opens the door, letting out warm air from the mini greenhouse inside. Following her in, I stretch like a cat in the heat of the sunlamps that turn this shack into a summer oasis.

Her escape from winter. I fill my lungs with a glorious blend of scents.

"Back here, Tyne."

Gran stands over a nasty black bush with twisted vines and thorns, like a tangle of barbed wire, now showing its first flowers. Her creeper roses have finally opened, revealing their color. The naturally ragged petals are a dark purple, almost black near the core.

"Every time I watched them wilt before they bloomed was like getting robbed of a present. I tried everything on them and nothing worked. But Jake gave me something that did the trick."

"What do you mean?"

"A special fertilizer, with a blend of ash, bone-meal and other nutrients. I spread it around here, and like magic my beautiful monsters finally opened their buds. I showed Jake how they bloomed. He said we should name it. I told him it wasn't a *new* flower variety, just a rare and difficult one. But Jake named it anyway."

"Named it what?"

She bends to smell one. "He called it Lucy."

37

THIS IS MY last chance.

The late combine, where the basketball scouts and university reps show up to see what you've got. A combination of workouts, drills and tests. All the girls who still haven't been signed or committed yet are here to show their stuff and get interviewed by recruiters for scholarships.

They take my measurements—height, weight, handspan, wingspan, feet, shoulder width and everything in between. There are the speed drills. Even when I hustle I'm one of the slowest in the sprints up and down the court. My reach is impressive, and the way I can palm the ball with my wide hands, but my vertical jump isn't wowing them.

And when it comes to the agility tests, my footwork can be clumsy. But nobody beats me in the strength tests, weight lifting, doing benches and squats. In the shootaround I do okay. But I don't pretend to be a shooter.

Mom roams the sidelines like an agent, talking me up to the scouts, bragging about my measurements and defensive game stats. She gets in an argument with one rep who says I'm more size than sizzle.

I have to tell her to chill. "Don't scrap with the scouts."

By the time the day is done I've had sweaty interviews with colleges across Canada and even some from the States.

Standing tall and looking fierce. Making sure nobody forgets Tiny.

MOM DOES MY bargaining. We want a full scholarship, guaranteed. Who knows how long my knee will last, so I need the insurance—of course we don't tell the schools that. But then I can graduate, and leave college with more than a limp.

Stick is in on my final push. He put together a video package of my high school highlights, cut together from footage shot by him and Dad over the past two seasons. We made a "top ten" of my best plays—blocks, rebounds and defensive battles that show off my skills. Me and Mom sent it to the reps.

Back on the court I'm a demon, muscling girls out of my way. Still waiting to hear from the colleges, I take out all my anger and frustration on the court. It feels good to be playing with the team again. But at the games something's missing. There's that empty seat where Dad used to sit.

When Stick was making my greatest-hits video, he found the footage from when I got hurt. My slam-dunk disaster. I've been watching it over and over, not to see what I did wrong, and not to torture myself. I watch it for what came after.

Stick shot me going airborne to make the dunk. When I come back down, I land ugly. My knee gives out and I hit the floor hard. I lie there, twisted in agony, holding my leg. The girls crowd around. Then a tall figure rushes onto the court and pushes through to my side. The camera is on us as Dad crouches next to me. I freeze the frame and I can see it all on his face. My pain mirrored there. His lips are moving, but the words are lost to me now. What matters most is the way his eyes hold mine, steady and firm, keeping me from being blinded by panic. He holds me together with the love in his look. Dad's the only one strong enough to pick me up and carry me off the court. Me and him, we know what it's like. To be big, to get hurt and get back up.

Me without him—I can't live with that.

So now I'm home after a game, and we're having dinner. I'm feasting on a tray of lasagna while everybody else shares a pizza. Mom's replaying the action for Dad, showing some highlights she shot on her tablet. I had a monster defensive double-double with nineteen rebounds and ten blocks.

Glancing up, I see him focused on the tablet in his hand. He's been keeping track of my game stats since the start, and I know he'll be adding tonight's to his file.

When dinner is done, Mom's cleaning up while Dad does dishes.

Now, while he's got his back to me at the kitchen sink, I force myself to speak.

"I missed you at the game tonight, Dad."

That stops him in rinsing off the plates. Mom looks over from the fridge, back and forth from me to him. There's just the sound of the water running till Dad clears his throat.

"Didn't know if you'd want me there," he says.

For a long moment it's like we're all holding our breath.

"I'm always going to want you there."

He glances over his shoulder at me, and it's all there on his face. He tries to speak, but there's so much that words can't say.

38

WHERE AM I going?

When you're trying to escape, all you think about is breaking out. Getting away. Once you make it out, what then?

When the offers came in I was stunned. Maybe I never really thought my plan would work, but I got callbacks from five colleges. Mom did the talking for me, looking for the best deal. Only two places were willing to give me a full scholarship. The others were spooked by my bad knee.

One university was on the West Coast, a world away, far from everything I've ever known. The other was the University of Toronto—just a subway ride from here.

So, do I say goodbye to everyone and run to the coast? Mom and Dad would never see me play, never see me at all. And what about Stick? I can't lose him, and I just got Dad back. But U of T is so close, would it be a real escape? How far is far enough?

I took a tour of the campus. It felt weird, like I was trespassing and they were going to call the cops to throw me out. It might only be next door, but it's a whole other universe.

I can be new again there, reinvent myself.

When I told everyone, I could feel how relieved they were.

So—the future. Stick's planning it out for me right now over at his place. We're eating Paradise pizzas after school in his room. I'm eating, he's ranting and raving.

"We could do some underground publicity for you. Guerilla marketing. Generate some buzz. Later, endorsement deals—shoes, fast food, fragrances."

I snort a laugh. "Nobody wants to smell like me. Not after running up and down the court all game. Besides, I'm never gonna go pro. I'll be lucky if my knee lasts a year. And you're not allowed to make money off playing college ball anyway."

"*You* can't make money off it. *I* can," he says with his goofy dreamer grin.

He pulls up a file on his laptop. "I even got a slogan for you, and a logo."

"Yeah, what's my slogan?"

Stick shows me the screen with a mock-up of a T-shirt that says TINY AIN'T TINY. Below that, there's a silhouette sketch of a tall figure with arms outstretched, a basketball in each hand.

"That's brilliant, Stick. You're my genius."

"Yeah. You could be a marketing monster."

I shake my head. Never going to happen, but I love seeing him all electric again, his blue eyes shining. He's not back to his old self, but some new self he's still figuring out. When he thinks about what happened to him he says it feels like a nightmare he can't believe was real, till he sees the scars on his face.

Stick's been dreaming and scheming for himself too. He scored a small scholarship. And Miss Diaz hustled him some government money—since he's a foster kid, a ward of the state, she got on them to help pay for his education.

He'll be taking courses at a community college in the fall—graphics and design.

"So, you gonna be an adman?"

"I can sell anything to anybody." He scoops up a slice of pizza and fills his face. "I sold you on me."

Bending down, I get a tomato-sauce kiss from him. "Wasn't a hard sell."

I finish off a bottle of Coke.

"There's more in the fridge," he says. "Get me one, would you?"

When I'm in the kitchen, the front door opens and Vega comes in. I've been so busy the past few weeks I haven't really talked to her—just "hi" in passing. Don't know what to say to her after what happened to Jake.

"Hey, Stretch."

"Vega."

I can smell the oil and exhaust on her. She's fresh from the garage in stained overalls, bandanna over her braids. She reaches under the sink for some hand-cleaner goop that gets oil and grease off better than soap.

"So you're gonna go to college?"

"Yeah. I got in."

Vega rubs the goop on her hands. "You done good."

"Guess so. Stick's doing good too, all healed up, back to his old self."

"Yeah, Miss Diaz babied him back. Gotta say, that boy can take a beating."

I don't want to ask, but I need to know.

"And my uncle—we don't have to worry about him anymore."

She nods, working the cleaner between her fingers and under her nails. "So I heard. Nasty accident. That's some tough luck. But when you go supercharging those old classic cars, putting too much power under the hood, and you don't know what you're dealing with, it can turn into a death trap. All it takes is the smallest defect to help it happen." Vega gives me a scary smile. "Screw around, and you're playing with fire."

That's as close to a confession as I'm going to get. Those icy eyes hold me still.

Then I break away, going in the fridge for some Coke.

"Yo, Stick," she calls. "You checked the chore chart? Says you're on laundry duty."

"Yeah, I know!" he shouts. "This afternoon."

"Get to it. You know Miss D runs a clean farm."

"I'm on it."

I head back to the bedroom. Stick's screening video of me pounding down the court like Godzilla attacking Tokyo, sweaty and red-faced.

"Look at me. What a beast."

"Yeah," he says, not taking it as a bad thing. "But you're beauty and the beast, all in one."

"And you're crazy." I dig my fingers into his porcupine curls, kissing his neck. "My kind of crazy."

39

THE ZOO SLEEPS beneath me.

I'm going to miss this view.

Standing on the roof, deep in the night, I look out at the millions of city lights, the millions of souls.

This is the place that made me.

I wander over to Gran's abandoned rooftop garden, bringing a ghost with me. When I was out to see her today she gave me a flower to take home. Lucy's rose.

I'm going to save it, dry the flower out to keep and remember. Not as another relic from a dead girl. I'll keep the rose as kind of a promise, to try to help if I find some other lost girl who needs it. I'll stand with her, and never back down.

If you want to get past me, you're going to have to move this giant.

Because that's what I do. It's what I *am*.

A defender.

ABOUT THE AUTHOR

GRAHAM MCNAMEE won the Edgar Award for *Accelera-tion*. He also wrote the thrillers *Bonechiller* and *Beyond*. A creature of the night, he lives in the dark.